“Thank you. But, so help me, David, if you come inside, I won’t get any work done.”

At that, he laughed. He leaned over, brushed his fingers down the side of her face, slowly moving over the curve of her cheek, along her jaw to her mouth, where he ran the pad of his thumb over her lips. “If that’s meant to scare me off, it’s not working.”

She dipped her head, rubbed her cheek along his fingertips. “It is your condo. I have no right to tell you when you can be here.”

“I’m not staying,” he said. She pushed the door open but didn’t move.

A gust of wind blew her hair into her face and she shoved it back. “Okay.”

“Unless you want me to.”

THE REBEL

USA TODAY **Bestselling Author**

ADRIENNE GIORDANO

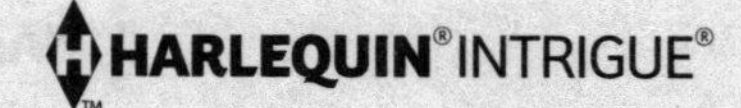

Recycling programs
for this product may
not exist in your area.

ISBN-13: 978-0-373-69865-3

The Rebel

This edition published by arrangement with Harlequin Books S.A.

For questions and comments about the quality of this book, please contact us at CustomerService@Harlequin.com.

Printed in U.S.A.

Adrienne Giordano, a *USA TODAY* bestselling author, writes romantic suspense and mystery. She is a Jersey girl at heart, but now lives in the Midwest with her workaholic husband, sports obsessed son and Buddy the wheaten terrorist (terrier). For more information on Adrienne's books, please visit adriennegiordano.com or download the Adrienne Giordano app. For information on Adrienne's street team, go to facebook.com/groups/dangerousdarlings.

Books by Adrienne Giordano

Harlequin Intrigue

The Prosecutor
The Defender
The Marshal
The Detective
The Rebel

CAST OF CHARACTERS

David Hennings—The "rebel" son of Pamela and Gerald Hennings. After years of living on his own in Boston, David moves back to Chicago to be closer to his family and is talked into helping solve a cold case involving an unidentified skull.

Amanda LeBlanc—An artist who specializes in sculpting, Amanda agrees to do a forensic sculpture on the skull of an unidentified murder victim.

Lawrence "Larry" McCall—The Chicago homicide detective who finds the buried skull of a murder victim. Detective McCall recruits Amanda to help identify the victim.

Penny Hennings—David's younger sister and a defense attorney with Hennings & Solomon. David hopes to rebuild a relationship with Penny after years of conflict between them.

Alexis "Lexi" Vanderbilt—Chicago's up-and-coming interior designer and Amanda's friend.

Jenna Hayward—A private investigator employed by Hennings & Solomon, Jenna is volunteered to help David and Amanda investigate.

Gerald Hennings—Senior partner of Hennings & Solomon and also David's father.

Pamela Hennings—David's mother and the socialite wife of Gerald Hennings who volunteers Hennings & Solomon's investigators to help solve cold cases.

Irene Dyce—Friend of the Henningses and the wife of a powerful activist. Mrs. Dyce agrees to use her political contacts to help David and Amanda identify the murder victim.

Chapter One

"Come on, boy. Another quarter mile and we're done."

Larry McCall whistled for Henry, his black Lab, who needed exercise more than Larry, to move along. Sunrise illuminated the sky, streaking it in shades of purple and orange that made even a grisly homicide detective marvel at the beauty of nature on an early fall morning.

With Henry busy sniffing a patch of dirt, Larry paused a moment, tilted his head back and inhaled the dewy air. Another two weeks, all these trees would be barren and the city would come in and scoop up the leaves. At which point, his body would make excuses to stay in bed rather than hoof it through ten acres of fenced-in fields on Chicago's southwest side.

Half expecting Henry to trot by him, Larry opened his eyes and glanced to his left, where the dog always walked. No Henry. Since when had he gotten subversive? Larry angled back and found Henry still at the spot he'd been sniffing a minute ago. Only now he was digging. Hard. Terrific. Not only would he have dirt all over him, but he'd also probably snatch a dead animal out of the ground and drop it at Larry's feet. *Here ya go, Dad.*

Not happening. He whistled again. "Leave it," he said in his best alpha-dog voice.

His bum luck was that Henry had alpha tendencies,

too, and kept digging. He'd have to leash him and pull him away before a dead squirrel wound up in his jaws.

Years earlier the city had torn down three low-income apartment buildings—the projects—because of the increased drug and criminal activity surrounding the place. All that was left was the fenced-in acreage that made for great walking. Problem was, there could be anything—rodents, needles, crack baggies, foil scraps—buried. *Needles. Dammit.* Larry hustled back to the dog before he got stuck. Or stoned.

"Whatever you found, Henry, we don't want any part of. Leave it."

He snapped the leash on, gently eased Henry back and was met with ferocious barking. What the hell? His happy dog had gone schizo.

"What is it, boy?"

Holding the dog off the hole he'd started, Larry bent at the waist to focus on something white—dull white—peeking through the dirt.

Henry barked and tugged at the leash.

"Okay, boy. Relax. Let me look at it."

He led a still-barking Henry to a tree, secured the leash around it to keep him at bay and walked back to the spot. Using the handkerchief he always carried—yes, he was that old-school, so what?—to protect his hands, he cleared more of the loose, moist dirt from the top, and more white appeared. He tapped the surface. Solid. Rock solid. And Larry's stomach twisted in a way it only did on the job.

Stop. Twenty years of working homicide told him he should. Right now. *Don't go any further; call it in.*

Birds chirped overhead, the sound so crisp and incessant it sliced right into his ears. Henry apparently had riled 'em good. Still squatting, Larry scanned the desolate area. Beyond the fence at the end of the last quarter mile, the early-morning rush began to swell on Cicero.

Henry barked again. Normally calm as a turtle, he wanted to dig.

Larry cocked his head to study whatever peeked through the dirt, and once again his stomach seized. After all these years, only one thing futzed with his stomach.

Crime scene.

But, truth be told, he had a tendency to overthink things. Something else years on the job had done to him. Hell, he could be staring at an old ceramic bowl. And how humiliating would it be to call this in and have it wind up being someone's china?

Just hell.

Henry barked again, urging him on, and Larry gave in to his curiosity and pushed more loose dirt around. At least until he hit a depression and his finger, handkerchief and all, slid right into it. Gently, he moved his finger around, hitting the outer edges of the depression, and a weird tingling shot up his neck. His breathing kicked up.

What'd this dog find?

He cleared more dirt, his fingers moving gently, revealing more and more of the surface of whatever was buried here. Once again, his fingers slipped into the depressed area and he knew. Dammit.

He'd just stuck his finger into an eye socket.

Chapter Two

Five Years Later

Surrounded by four hundred guests, seven of them sitting at her table in the ballroom of Chicago's legendary Drake Hotel, Amanda studied a giant photo of a fallen firefighter that had flashed on the screen behind the podium. Without a doubt, she'd botched his nose.

Ugh. How embarrassing. Any novice artist, particularly a sculptor, would see the slight flare of the man's nostrils. She slid her gaze to the sculpture, her sculpture, a gift to the widow of Lieutenant Ben Broward, who'd died three months ago after running into a crumbling building to save a child.

The child had survived.

Ben had not.

And Amanda's gift to his widow and their children was now worthless. At least in Amanda's mind. Had the flaring nostrils been that obvious on the photos she'd been given? Later, when she arrived home, she'd swing into her studio and check. Just to satisfy herself.

Darn it.

Sitting back in her chair, she eased out a breath and made eye contact with Lexi, her interior designer friend who'd originally suggested she attend this fund-raiser and meet Pamela Hennings and Irene Dyce, both politically connected—and extremely wealthy—women. Amanda's idea to donate the sculpture had come after seeing an interview with Lieutenant Broward's wife and children. She couldn't give them the man back, but maybe the sculpture would bring some sort of peace. Not exactly closure because Amanda didn't buy in to that whole closure thing. What did that even mean? Tragedy was tragedy and she doubted Ben's family would ever fully recover.

Mrs. Hennings leaned closer to speak over the chatter and the sound of clanging silverware filling the room. "Amazing likeness, dear."

"Yes," Mrs. Dyce said from the other side of Mrs. Hennings. "Beautiful work, Amanda."

"Thank you."

Not that she believed it after spotting her mistake, but coming from Mrs. Hennings, the wife of Chicago's most brilliant defense attorney, a woman notorious for her good taste, Amanda, as she always did, graciously accepted the compliment, allowing it to momentarily smother her doubt.

At least until she looked at that nose again. Would the widow notice? Would she see the blunder every time she chose to look at the piece? Would it drive her insane? Gah.

The woman couldn't spend years looking at a nose butchered by the artist. Amanda couldn't allow it. She'd redo the piece. That was all. She'd make time to fix her mistake.

Done.

Over.

Move on.

A waiter slid a slice of cherry cheesecake in front of her. Any other day, she'd happily indulge, which of course wouldn't help her lose that extra ten pounds, but a girl had a right to sugar. Simple fact. But after the beating she'd just given herself, she wasn't sure her stomach could handle a rich dessert. Gently, she nudged the plate away, opting instead for a sip of water.

"Evening, Miss LeBlanc."

She glanced up to where a large, barrel-chested man, late fifties perhaps, stood behind her. "Hello."

"I'm Detective Larry McCall. Chicago PD. Homicide." He gestured to the vacant chair next to her. "Mind if I sit?"

Oh, boy. What was this?

Whatever it was, she was thankful he wasn't the man who'd been sitting beside her all evening. *That* man, a financial planner from one of the city's big banks, had disappeared more than thirty minutes ago after she flatly told him, no, she was not interested in doing "hot" things in his bed. What an idiot. With any luck, he'd found a woman willing to take him up on his offer.

She held her hand out. "Of course. Someone was sitting there, but he's been gone awhile."

Hopefully, for good.

The detective glanced across the table to where Lexi sat with her boyfriend, Brodey, another Chicago homicide detective and also the brother of one of the Hennings & Solomon investigators. Seemed to Amanda that the Hennings clan had a connection to just about everyone in this city.

"Junior," Detective McCall said, nodding a greeting.

"Lawrence," Brodey drawled.

And how amusing was this? Clearly these two were in some kind of twisted male peeing match, and Amanda did everything in her power not to roll her eyes.

Detective McCall dropped his bulky frame into the chair beside her. "I'll move if he comes back. Sorry if I'm interrupting."

"Not at all. What can I do for you, Detective?"

"I checked out your bust."

Amanda bit her lip, stifling a smile as the detective replayed in his mind the last seconds—wait for it. *There.*

He smacked himself on the head, then did it again, but he laughed at himself all the same. Instantly she liked him, liked his ability to find humor in embarrassing situations, liked his acceptance of his blunder without making a fuss.

"I apologize," he said. "This is what happens when you put a guy like me in a place like this. I insult nice women."

And he had the rough-around-the-edges grit of one of those throwback detectives she liked to watch on reruns of *NYPD Blue*.

"Well," she said, "lucky for you I'm not easily offended. And what's worse is that I figured out immediately you meant the sculpture and not my—" she looked down, circled her hand in front of her chest "—you know."

"The sculpture. Yeah. It's really good."

Aside from the botched nose.

"Thank you."

"No. I mean it's *really* good. I knew Ben. Good guy. Great guy, actually. His wife is the daughter of..." He shook his head, waved it off. "Never mind. Doesn't matter. The sculpture is...accurate. Scary accurate."

Hmm... Having been approached by detectives before, Amanda felt the puzzle pieces beginning to come together and she readied herself to ruin Detective McCall's evening. “I had a few photos from different angles to work from.”

“Yeah, I guess that helps. Listen, do you ever do forensic work?”

And there it was.

As suspected, the detective wanted her help on a case. Probably doing an age progression on a missing child or working with a witness to identify an attacker. Because of budgeting woes and a lack of funds for full-time forensic artists, police departments sometimes hired outside the department.

None of it mattered. She’d have to turn him down. “I’m sorry, Detective. I do have an interest and have taken some classes, but it’s not work I feel comfortable with yet.”

McCall, apparently ignoring her refusal, leaned in. “I’ve got this case…”

He has a case. On countless occasions throughout her childhood she’d heard those very words from her mother, a part-time forensic artist. Amanda held her hand up. “I’d like to help, but I have little experience in forensic work. I’d do more harm than good.”

“No, you wouldn’t. Trust me. It’s a cold case. Five years now. No leads. All we have is a skull and some hairs found where it was dug up. That’s all that’s left of her.”

“Her?”

“The medical examiner thinks it’s a female. Maybe late teens or early twenties.”

“I see.”

“I actually found her.”

Amanda gawked. Couldn’t help it. “You found the skull?”

The detective shook his head as he let out a huff. “Craziest damned thing. I was out walking my dog in that vacant spot near Midway, and Henry started digging. I'll never forget it. Whoever this girl is, she and I are a team. I made sure I kept her case. It's mine."

"That's admirable, Detective. Really."

He shrugged. "We have a sketch done by one of the department artists, but I don't know. Maybe she got it wrong because no one is coming forward to claim this girl and we didn't get any hits from DNA. I'm a father. It makes me sick." He ran his hand over his thinning, gray hair as he scanned the ballroom and the people moving toward the exit. "I saw what you did with the sculpture of Ben and thought maybe you could help us out."

Amanda glanced across at Lexi, hoping to grab her attention with the *save me* stare. No luck there because her friend was busy whispering in Brodey's ear. By the look on his face, he liked what he was hearing. A flash of something whipped inside Amanda. At odd times, she missed the comfort, the familiarity, the *knowing* of an exclusive relationship. Casual dating didn't provide any of that.

But a pity party wouldn't get her assistance from Lexi or Brodey. To her right, Mrs. Hennings and Mrs. Dyce were in deep conversation about scheduling a lunch, so there'd be no help there, either. For this one, she'd fly solo. Try once again to nicely let the detective know she couldn't help him. As much as she felt for him, she wouldn't—couldn't—risk involvement. She faced him again, meeting his gaze straight on. "Detective, I'm sorry. It's just not what I do. I've never done a reconstruction before. I could ask around, though, and see if any of my colleagues might be interested."

McCall hesitated and studied her eyes for a few seconds, apparently measuring her resolve. He must have received her message because he nodded, his jowly cheeks shaking with the effort. "I'd appreciate that. Thank you. I want to give this girl her name back."

And, oh, that made Amanda's stomach burn. Ten years ago, her mother would have loved this project.

A lot had changed in ten years.

Movement from Amanda's right drew her attention to Mrs. Hennings placing her napkin on the table. "I'm sorry to say, it's past my bedtime." Mrs. Hennings touched Mrs. Dyce's shoulder. "I'll call you in the morning and we'll figure out a day for lunch."

"I'll be at the youth center. Call me there."

"Will do." Mrs. Hennings nodded at Lexi. "And I'll have David call *you* about his new home. He needs help. Just don't tell him I said that."

Lexi laughed. "Your secret is safe with me. And thank you. I'm excited to work with him."

Then Mrs. Hennings turned her crystal-blue gaze on Amanda. "My son has just moved back from Boston. Lexi will be helping him on the redesign of his condominium. I'd love to have him look at your artwork. He's starting from scratch." Her lips lifted into a calculating smile only mothers pulled off. "Whether he likes it or not, he's starting from scratch."

And from what Amanda had heard from Lexi, when Mrs. Hennings made a request, you should not be fool enough to deny her. When it came to Chicago's upper crust, Mrs. Hennings might be their president.

"Of course," Amanda said. "I'd love to. Lexi and I have worked together several times. Your son can come by my studio and look at some of my paintings. Or we could do a sculpture. Whatever he likes."

The older woman reached to shake Amanda's hand. "Wonderful. I'll have him call you."

"OH, COME ON, David," Mom said. "I know you can be charming."

David Hennings sat in the kitchen of his parents' home, his hand wrapped around a steaming mug of coffee, and faced down his mother, a woman so formidable and connected the mayor of Chicago kept in constant communication with her. She might be able to sway masses, but she was still his mother and, at times, needed to be told no.

Otherwise, she'd control him.

And that wasn't going to happen.

"Mom, thank you for your never-ending encouragement."

She scoffed at his sarcasm. "You know what I mean."

Yes, he did. As much as he liked the usual banter between them, he didn't want to hear about whatever scheme she had going. Not on a Monday morning when he had a to-do list a mile long, including meeting with the contractor renovating his new condo. Yep, after two weeks of living under his parents' roof, because even he couldn't be rebellious enough to break his mother's heart by staying in a hotel, he needed to get that condo in shape so he could move in.

As usual, Mom kept her piercing eyes on him and with each second she slowly, methodically chipped away at him. This look was famous in the Hennings household. *This* look could possibly bring down an entire nation. He blew air through his lips, part of his willpower going with it. "Have you talked to Dad about this?"

"Of course."

Lying. He eyed her.

"Well, I mentioned it. In passing."

David snorted. "I thought so."

After attending a fund-raiser for a fireman's fund the night before, his mother had gotten it into her head that Hennings & Solomon, the law firm his father had founded, should have their investigators look into a cold case. An apparent homicide. All in all, David didn't get what she wanted from him. All she knew about the case was what she'd overheard at the dinner table. One, some detective had a skull he couldn't identify. Two, the detective wanted a sculptor to do a reconstruction.

That was it.

A reconstruction alone would be no easy task if an artist didn't have training in forensics. And who knew what kind of credentials this particular artist had?

David might not have been a criminal lawyer like his father and siblings, but he knew that much about forensics.

Mom folded her arms and leaned one hip against the counter. "We can help. I know we can."

For years now, the two of them had been allies. Unlike his siblings, when David needed shelter, he went to his mother. He adored her, had mad respect for her. No matter what. Through that hellish few months when he'd destroyed his father's dream of his oldest son joining the firm because David had decided civil law—horrors!—might be the way to go, his mother had pled David's case, tirelessly arguing that he needed to be his own man and make his own decisions.

And Dad had given in.

It might have been butt-ugly, but the man had let David go.

That was the power of Pamela Hennings.

David slugged the last of his coffee because, well, at this point, the extra caffeine couldn't hurt.

"Okay," he said. "You do realize I'm not a criminal

attorney, right? And, considering I don't even work at Hennings & Solomon, I'm guessing I'm not the guy for this assignment."

"Your father said Jenna and the other investigator, Mike what's-his-name, are too busy. And *you* said you were bored. Since your new office won't be ready for a couple of weeks, you can do this. *We* can do this."

Cornered. Should have known she had a counterattack prepped. So like his mother to use his own words against him after he'd complained the night before that the contractor doing the renovation on his new office was running behind. Had he known that, he'd have stayed in Boston another two weeks before packing up and moving home to open his own firm.

"But I'm meeting with my contractor this morning."

"By the way, as soon as you're done with him, you need to call Lexi."

"The decorator? Why?"

Mom huffed and gave him the dramatic eye roll that had won lesser actresses an Academy Award. "Interior designer, dear. And what do you mean, why? I told you I arranged for her to work with you. Because, so help me, David, you will not be living the way you did in Boston with all that oddball furniture and no drapes. You, my love, are a grown man living like a teenager. Besides, Lexi's significant other knows the detective from last night. When you talk to Lexi, get the detective's name. He'll help you. We'll get Irene Dyce in on this, as well." Mom waggled her hand. "She was at the fund-raiser last night and overheard the conversation. I'm about to call her to set up lunch and you can bet I'll mention it. Between her and her husband, they know half this city. It's doable, David."

He sat forward and pinched the bridge of his nose. By now he should be used to this. The bobbing and weaving his mother did to confuse people and get them to relent. "What is it exactly you want me to do?"

She slapped a business card in front of him. "Talk to the artist. I got her card last night. I told her you were about to move into a new home and might need artwork."

"Seriously? You're tricking her? And how much is *that* going to cost me?"

"David Jeremy Hennings, just shush. I needed a reason to contact her again. And it's not a trick if you hire her. Just have her do a painting or something. That's only fair."

If he wound up buying something, his mother was paying for it. That was all he knew. Sighing, he picked up the card. Amanda LeBlanc. Nice name. Good, solid name. "Why do I need to talk to her?"

"She told the detective she couldn't do the sculpture. I think she's intrigued, though. She might just need a push. And you, my darling, excel at the art of the push."

He held up both hands. "Mom, please don't strain yourself with all these compliments. First I'm charming, and now it's persuasive. This might all go to my head."

"You need to zip it with the sass. For God's sake, you're the intellectual around here. You love research and history and combing through information to reach a conclusion. This case would be perfect for you."

"I'm no investigator."

"But you don't have to be. All you need to do is get the ball rolling. Think of the people we have at our disposal. Russ is an FBI agent. I'm sure he'd help."

Now she wanted to drag his sister's boyfriend into this. Great. Given David's strained—as in they drove each other nuts—relationship with Penny, he and Russ hadn't gotten off to the greatest of starts.

Inspired, Mom boosted herself away from the counter and sat in the chair beside his. *It's over now.* When she got charged up like this, there'd be no denying her.

"David, I want you to think about this. You moved back to Chicago to be part of this family again."

"Mom—"

"Shush. I love you, but you've always had an issue with feeling like the odd man out."

Damn, she's good.

"If you'd really like to be included in all those nasty dinner conversations about criminal cases, this is the way to start. So far, the firm's quasi cold-case squad has solved two murders. Two, David. Do you know how many nights I've had to listen to your father, Zac and Penny rehash those cases?" She held up her hand. "A lot. This is your chance to finally be part of the conversation. And, frankly, I want this. For the first time, I get to be part of the conversation, too, and I like it. I'm not your father's socialite wife anymore. I'm more than an *appendage*."

Academy Award winner Pamela Hennings. "Cut that out. You've never been an appendage. He's terrified of you. Everyone knows that."

"Everyone knows I'm his wife and that, yes, we have a strong relationship, but I've never had a job, David. All the charity work and clubs, it's all an offshoot of your father's work. Not that I haven't enjoyed it, but if given the chance at a redo, I'd have a career of my own. Doing what, I don't know. All I know is that I'm suddenly someone who can help bring justice and it's not because it's expected of me. So buck up and do this for your mother."

Game over. She'd turned the entire thing around on him, playing up the guilt because she knew, when it came to her, he rarely said no. Damn. How the hell did she always do this? He ticked through the conversation, then burst out laughing.

"What's funny?"

He grabbed his cup, rose from his chair and kissed her on the cheek. "Nothing. You're brilliant. You've totally manipulated me into doing this. And I let you. Being around lawyers has rubbed off on you."

"You'll do it?"

"I'll talk to the artist. Then I'm done. I'm not an investigator and have no interest in being one. I have a law practice to open."

Mom pushed up from the table and held her index fingers up. "That's fine. Talk her into at least doing the reconstruction. You're better at that sort of thing than I am. Once you convince her, I'll handle it from there."

"I'm sure you will, Mom. I'm sure you will."

"And, by the way, dinner is at seven-thirty tonight. Zac and Emma will be here and Russ and Penny."

She ran her gaze over his clothes, starting at his long-sleeved henley. He knew she hated the Levi's jeans and boots, but he wasn't five anymore and didn't need his mother dressing him. "Don't start, Mom."

"Between the clothes and that facial hair, I have to ask that you not come to the table dressed like you escaped from prison."

Facial hair. She acted as if he had a hobo beard rather than the close-cropped one he favored. He snatched his favorite leather jacket, the one with the intricate stitching on the shoulders, off the back of his chair, and Mom's lips peeled back. "Mom, this is a two-thousand-dollar jacket. Besides, my *tux* is at the dry cleaner's."

"Don't be fresh."

More than done with this conversation, he shrugged into his coat. "I've gotta go. You've convinced me to talk to this artist. I love you, but quit while you're ahead."

Chapter Three

Morning sun shifted, the light angling sideways instead of straight into Amanda's studio, and she stepped back from the sculpture. She'd been messing with the lips of a cell-phone manufacturer's CEO, bending the clay, tweaking and retweaking for two hours, and she still couldn't get the mouth right. And worse, she couldn't figure out why. As much as it irritated her, drove her to near madness, it didn't matter. She'd keep at it. No matter how long it took. After the botched nose on the fireman, resulting in a shake-up of her confidence, she'd get these lips perfect.

The changing sunlight through the loft's oversize windows didn't help, so she adjusted the six-foot lamp behind her, directing the light in a more favorable position. Light, light and more light helped keep her focused for the sometimes tedious hours spent in front of a sculpture. Changing shadows meant time slipping from her greedy hands. She glanced at the clock. Eleven thirty. She'd been at it six hours, two of them lost on bum lips.

"Okay, girlfriend. You need to get it together here. Forget the nose. It's one nose. It shouldn't be a career-ending mistake."

Intellectually, she knew it. Emotionally, that faulty nose might do her in.

The studio phone rang, filling the quiet space with its annoying blinging sound. Typically, she'd ignore the phone until her exhausted and sore fingers gave out for the day. But now, with the rotten lips, it was probably a good time to take a break. Grab a quick lunch and refocus. She scooted to her desk in the corner and snatched up the handset.

"Good morning. This is Amanda."

"Good morning, Amanda. My name is David Hennings. You met my mother at an event last night."

And, hello, sexy voice of my dreams. Wow. The low-pitched resonance of that voice poured over her. With her dating history, he was probably five inches shorter than her and a total mama's boy. "Hello, Mr. Hennings. I did meet your mother last night. She's a lovely dinner companion."

For whatever reason, he laughed at that, the sound just as yummy as his voice.

"That she is," he said. "She told me she mentioned I was moving into a new place."

Seriously, he didn't sound short. Or like a mama's boy. If that even made sense because how could anyone know what someone looked like by the way he spoke? She had a vision, though. A good one, an exceptional one, of a tall man, fair haired and blue-eyed like his mother. And he'd wear suits every day. Slick, Italian suits that alerted the world to his blue-blood status. Yes indeed, she had a vision.

"She mentioned you'd be working with Lexi, who is a friend, by the way. Would you like to set up an appointment and we can discuss what you might need?"

"Definitely. I just spoke with Lexi. I could swing by. If you're available."

"Now?"

"If that works. Otherwise, we could look at tomorrow."

Apparently Mrs. Hennings was in a hurry. Amanda swung back to her sculpture and the stubborn lips. A break might help. Discussing new projects always seemed to cleanse the palate, help her look at existing work with fresh perspective and excitement. But she wasn't exactly dressed to meet a new client. Knowing she had a full day of sculpting ahead, she'd yanked her hair into a ponytail and slipped on her baggiest of baggy jeans and a "Make Love, Not War" T-shirt a friend had given her as a joke. The hair she could deal with by removing her hair band. The clothes? Not so much.

"Mr. Hennings, that would be fine. But I have to warn you, I'm working on a sculpture today and when I sculpt I dress comfortably. I didn't expect to have a meeting."

"Don't worry about it. I'm in jeans. My mother is on a mission, Amanda, and if you know my mother at all, you know that if I tell her I didn't meet with you because of what you were wearing, she'll skin me."

"So you're saying you're afraid of your mother."

"I'm not *afraid* of my mother. I'm *terrified of her*."

For the first time all day, considering the lips, Amanda laughed. A good, warm one that made her toes curl. Any argument she'd had to avoid meeting with him today vanished when he'd dropped that line about his mother. Simply put, she loved a grown man who understood his mother's power. How that grown man handled that power was a different story. Heaven knew she'd dated some weaklings, men who not only were afraid of their mothers, but also let them dictate how their lives should go. That, on a personal level, Amanda couldn't deal with. On a professional level, she didn't necessarily care as long as her fee got paid.

Besides, she liked David Hennings. She liked the

sound of his voice even more. Call it curiosity, a mild interest in meeting a man with a voice like velvet against skin, but she wanted to check him out.

"Okay, Mr. Hennings. You can come by now."

"Great. I'll see you soon. And it's David."

INSIDE THE STAIRWELL of the hundred-year-old building on the city's West Side, David climbed the last few steps leading to the landing of Amanda's second-floor studio. He loved these old structures with the Portland stone and brick. The iconic columns on the facade urged the history major in him to research the place. Check the city records, see what information he could find on who'd built it, who'd lived here or which companies had run their wares through its doors.

Structures like this had a charm all their own that couldn't be duplicated with modern wizardry. Old buildings, this building, had a life, a past to be researched and appreciated.

Or maybe he just wanted to believe that.

He rapped on the door. No hollow wood there. By the scarred look and feel of its heavy weight under his knuckles, it might be the original door. How amazing would *that* be?

The door swung open and a woman with lush curves a guy his size could wrap himself around greeted him. She wore jeans and a graphic T-shirt announcing he should make love, not war—*gladly, sweetheart*—and her honey-blond hair fell around her shoulders, curling at the ends. The whole look brought thoughts of lazy Sunday mornings, hot coffee and a few extracurricular activities, in a bed and out, David could think of.

To say the least, she affected him.

And she hadn't even opened her mouth. *Please don't be an airhead.*

"David?"

Yep. That was the voice from earlier. Soft and sweet and stirring up all kinds of images right along with Sunday mornings and coffee. With any luck, more than the coffee would be hot.

Hokay. Mission Pam Hennings getting derailed by wicked thoughts. Time to get serious.

"Hi. Amanda?"

"Yes." She held her hand out. "Amanda LeBlanc."

David grasped her hand and glanced down at her long, elegant fingers folding over his. Her silky skin absorbed his much larger hand, and he might like to stay this way awhile. Nice hands. Soft hands. He'd imagined a sculptor's hands to be work-hardened and rough. Not that she swung an ax all day, but he'd expected…different.

"Um." She pointed at their still joined hands. "I kinda need that hand back."

Epic fail, Dave. He grinned and regrettably slid his hand away. "Don't take this the wrong way, but where have you been all my life?"

As recoveries went, it wouldn't be listed among the top hundred in brilliance, but a man had to work with what he had. Still, her lips, those extraordinary, shapely lips, twisted until she finally gave up and awarded him with a smile.

"Good one," she said. "Come inside and we'll talk about your project."

Right to business. Couldn't blame her. She didn't know him and he'd not only barged in on her day, but also hit on her. He stepped into the loft and let out a low whistle. A few walls had obviously been knocked out because her studio took up half of the entire floor. He scanned the room, his eyes darting over the open ceiling, the gleaming white walls, the easels and canvases in one corner. A large table covered with tools and brushes separated one area from a second space, where a bust was mounted on an adjustable stand.

She closed the door behind him. "I'd ask you to excuse the mess, but since it always looks like this, I won't bother."

"It's a studio. I'm not sure it's supposed to be neat."

"We can talk over here." She motioned him to a round table for four by the windows.

"This is a great space. Fantastic light. Do you know anything about the building?"

Her eyebrows dipped. "As in who owns it?"

"No. Sorry. I'm a history buff. Majored in it in college. The columns out front make me think early 1900s architecture."

"Ah. A man after my own heart. Believe it or not, I'm the only tenant right now. People just don't see the beauty. According to city records, it was constructed in 1908. I'm not sure my landlord has a clue what a gem he has. When I toured the building he told me he wanted to paint the front of it."

David opened his mouth, but nothing came out.

"I know," she said. "I had to give him the number of a company that specializes in stone cleaning and repair before he stripped the historical value out of the place."

"No kidding."

Amanda took the chair by the window, where a legal pad and pencil waited to be put to use. David slid his jacket off, set it on the chair next to his and sat across from her. Damn, the woman was gorgeous. All big brown eyes and soft cheeks to go with the healthy curves.

"Is that jacket a Belstaff?" she asked.

And, oh, oh, oh, she knew motorcycles. Or at least biker jackets. This expedition of his mother's might make his day.

"It is. You like motorcycles?"

"My dad does. What do you ride?"

"A Ducati. Diavel Carbon." He smiled. "It's a *beast*."

"It should be with a name like Diavel. You know what it means, right?"

He sure did. "*Diavolo.* Italian for devil."

She grinned. "And are you? A devil?"

"My mother would say I am. *I* think I'm a history nerd with a thing for motorcycles."

"Huh," she said.

"What?"

"Nothing. You're just not what I expected."

Now, this sounded good. Maybe. "You know I have to ask…"

"I expected someone who looks like your mother. Tall, blond hair, Italian suit. Instead I got dark with an Italian motorcycle."

He bit his bottom lip, then ran his teeth over it. "If my brother had knocked on your door, you'd have nailed it." He shrugged. "But hey, you got the tall part right."

"That's something, I guess."

She picked up her pencil and tossed her hair over her shoulder and David's pulse went berserk. Damn, this woman was beautiful. And not in the normal way. This was more corn-fed, casual beauty that she probably had no idea she possessed.

She angled her notepad in front of her. "Anyway, tell me about this project. What kind of paintings are you looking for?"

Nudes.

Of her.

His mother would castrate him. He cleared his throat and got *that* vision out of his head. The naked Amanda, not the castration. But the castration was no picnic, either.

But here was where this scenario got sticky because his sneaky mother, God bless her, had taken Amanda's card under the guise of providing him with art for his condo. Well, he'd get the art anyway because he would not waste this woman's time under false pretenses. "I'm not sure. I was thinking maybe we could work with Lexi on that. Something bold, deep colors. I don't know. It's not my thing. That's why I have Lexi."

"She's good at it, that's for sure. I can call her. Then I'll pull some paintings I think will work. If you don't like them, maybe I can create something specific for you."

Which, lucky him, would give him another reason to show up and maybe convince the lovely Amanda LeBlanc to have dinner with him. "That'll work. I have another project that my mother is interested in."

Amanda's eyebrows hitched up. No surprise there. His mother was notorious for spending big bucks on decorating. And landing her as a client would open a lot of doors when it came to an artist's career.

"What does she have in mind?"

"A sculpture."

"Oh, my specialty. Who will the sculpture be of?"

Here we go. "We don't know."

She laughed. "That's a new one. All right. I'll play. How do we find out who this sculpture will be of?"

Okay. So apparently his mother hadn't said anything—at all—to Amanda about her interest in the cold case discussed at the fund-raiser the night before. She'd totally set him up, and he'd give her an earful about that. When he showed up wearing jeans and *facial hair* at dinner.

That'd teach her. "Did my mother say anything to you about my father's law firm and their side work?"

"No."

Thanks, Mom. This right here might be one of the reasons he'd moved to Boston four years ago. Keeping up with the Hennings family shenanigans and the constant arguing and petty competition with Penny made his brain hurt. So he'd taken off. Got himself breathing room halfway across the country. *Welcome home, kid.*

"My dad is the founding partner of Hennings & Solomon."

"David, everyone in this city knows who your dad is."

True. "Right. Last fall my mom convinced him to have one of the firm's investigators work on a pro bono case. A cold case."

Amanda sat forward and waved her pencil. "I read about that. It involved a US Marshal or something."

"That's the one. His mother was murdered and the case, up to that point, was unsolved. The firm's investigator looked into it, and between her and the victim's son, they solved the case."

"Yes! I remember reading about it. Fascinating."

Glad you think so. That would only help when he ambushed her with doing this skull reconstruction his mother was so bent on. "Then my mother found another case she wanted to help solve."

"Your mother is a busy woman."

Honey, you have no idea. "She is. And her instincts are spot-on because the firm managed to help solve that one, too."

"How wonderful for her. And the firm's investigator must be excellent at what she does."

"She is. But she's had help. Cases like this take work

and she comes from a family of detectives with major contacts."

Amanda sat up straighter, pencil still at the ready, but her body language—stiff shoulders, pressed lips—went from curious to defensive. The temperature in the room might have plummeted to negative numbers.

This was it. Headfirst. Right here. "My mother overheard your conversation with the detective last night. The one with the unidentified skull."

She dropped her pencil and pushed the pad away. She held her hands up and sucked in her cheeks, the look hard and unyielding, transforming her from the lush sex kitten he wanted his hands on to a woman set for battle.

Where the hell *had* she been all his life?

"No," she said.

"I'm afraid my mother has you on her radar. And you're locked on."

"She'll have to unlock me, then. I explained to the detective last night that I couldn't do the sculpture. I have limited, insanely limited, experience with forensic sculptures. I've taken a couple of workshops, but I've never attempted a forensic reconstruction. I'm simply not qualified."

"If you've never tried, how do you know you can't do it?"

She set her palms flat on the table, the tips of her fingers burrowing into the wood and turning pink. "David, I'm sorry. Tell your mother I appreciate her following up on this, but my answer is no. It would be a waste of everyone's time. The painting for your new home, I'd be happy to do."

"Great. But indulge me on the reconstruction for a second."

Amanda huffed out a breath, half laughing but not really. In a way, he felt bad for her. He knew exactly how pushy the Hennings bunch could be. "Trust me," he said. "I feel your pain."

"Are you a lawyer like the rest of your family?"

"I am."

"Knew it. You have that lawyer tenacity."

He grinned. "I'm civil law. Everyone else is on the criminal side. But since I have that lawyer tenacity, I'd like to make you a deal."

"No."

Time to try a different approach because he wanted a dinner date with this woman and he liked sparring with her. Even if she didn't know either of those things.

Yet.

He sat forward, angled his head toward the sculpture across the room and pointed. "Looking at that, I'd say you're a talented woman."

"Thank you. And nice try."

She folded her arms, visually ripping holes into his body, and the twisted side of him, the strategizer, loved it. "You're welcome. What we have here is a detective trying to identify a body. A body deserving of a proper burial. Someone whose family is probably wondering what happened to their loved one."

"David—"

"Even if you don't think you have the experience, what would it hurt to try? I mean, this is fairly specialized work. I can't imagine there are a ton of forensic sculptors in this city."

"It would be a waste of everyone's time."

"I'll pay you."

Her head dipped. "You'll pay me to attempt a sculpture that may or may not serve a purpose?"

Apparently so. And that was news to him, too, but

he'd gotten on a roll, so why not? Cost of doing business when it came to keeping his mother off his back. "Yes. The worst-case scenario is that no one will identify the person. Best case is your sculpture helps the police figure out what happened, brings someone home and puts their family out of misery. And you'll get paid. I don't see the downside."

IF HE WANTED a downside, she could give him one. One so huge that if this project failed, and it could fail in any number of ways, she might find herself emotionally debilitated for years. Having an acute sense of her own emotional awareness, Amanda chose to avoid situations involving someone else's future. She'd learned that lesson from her now-deceased mother.

She drew in a breath and thought about the bright spring morning ten years ago when her mother had swallowed a bottle of pills. Amanda reminded herself—as if it ever went away—what it had felt like to touch Mom's lifeless body. Before that day, she'd never known just how cold a body could get.

Right now that memory kept her focused on convincing the extremely handsome and determined man across from her just how stubborn she could be. From the moment she'd opened the studio door, David Hennings had surprised her. Not only did he not look a thing like his mother, but he also didn't dress like any blue blood she'd ever met. If the chiseled face, sexy dark beard and enormous shoulders weren't enough, the man rode a big, bad motorcycle known to be one of the fastest production bikes out there. That beauty did zero to sixty in less than three seconds, and something told her David Hennings loved to make it scream.

Mentally, she fanned herself. Cooled her own firing

engines because…well…*wow. Stay strong, girlfriend.* She'd always had a thing for a man on a motorcycle. She sat back, casually crossed her legs and wished she weren't wearing ratty jeans. "David, trust me—there's a downside to this kind of work. People are sent to prison based on an artist's sketch. I don't want that responsibility." She waved her hand around the studio. "I want to paint and sculpt for my clients' enjoyment."

He nodded, but he obviously wasn't done yet. She saw it in the way he stared at her, his dark blue eyes so serious but somehow playful, as well. Whatever this was, he was enjoying it.

And between his height and his shoulders, he filled her sight line. Amazing that a man this imposing could come from a woman as petite as Mrs. Hennings. Then again, he'd clearly inherited his media-darling father's big-chested build. A few wisps of his collar-length hair, such a deep brown it bordered on black, fell across his forehead and he pushed them back, resting his long fingers against his head for a second, almost demanding those hairs stay put. Amanda's girlie parts didn't just tingle, they damn near sizzled.

Whew.

The object of her indecent thoughts gestured to the piece she'd worked on that morning. "May I?"

"Of course."

He took his time getting to the sculpture, his gaze on it as he moved, and Amanda's skin caught fire. Prowling, sexual energy streamed from him as he contemplated her work, head cocked one way and then the other, that strong jaw so perfect she'd love to sculpt it.

And her without a fan.

"What do you think?" she asked.

"I think your work is exceptional. And I'm not saying that because I want something from you." He smiled. "Certain lines I won't cross, and doling out high praise when it's not warranted is one of them."

"Thank you. I take it you like art?"

He shrugged. "I like to study things. To research them. Like this building. I saw it and had to know its history."

"All right, what do you see in that sculpture?"

"The mouth." He went back to the photo on the stand. "It's not quite there yet."

Amazing. "I worked on the lips all morning. Something isn't right."

Now he looked back at her, a full-on smile exploding across his face, and Amanda's lungs froze. Just stopped working. To heck with Michelangelo, Amanda LeBlanc now had a David of her very own.

"I have another deal for you."

Her lungs released and she eased out a breath. "You're full of deals today."

"I'm a lawyer. It's what I do."

"Fine. What's your deal?"

"I'll tell you what the problem is with your sculpture if you go with me to see this detective."

Moving closer, she kept her gaze on him and the not-too-smug curve of his mouth. "You know what's wrong with the lips?"

"I believe I do."

As a trained artist, one with a master's in fine arts, she'd spent hours trying to figure it out, and now the history major thought he knew. Oh, this was so tempting. She'd love to prove him wrong and knock some of that arrogance right out of him. But, darn. The way he carried that confidence, that supreme knowing made her stomach pinch.

"What's wrong, Amanda? Cat got your tongue?"

And *ohmygod*, he was *such* a weasel. A playful weasel, but still. She snorted. "Please. The cat having my tongue has never been an issue. Perhaps I'm merely stunned by your gigantic ego."

"Oh, harsh." He splayed his hand and his beautifully long fingers over his chest, but his face gave him away, all those sharp angles softly curving when he smiled. "You wound me."

Such a weasel. From her worktable, she grabbed her flat wooden tool. "Okay, hotshot. Let's see what you've got."

"If I tell you and it works, you go with me to see that detective. That's the deal."

"Yes. If it works, I'll go with you."

Silly, silly girl. All this to prove him wrong. Something told her, if he nailed this, she might never hear the end of it.

He smiled at her, spun to the sculpture and, without touching it, pointed to the right corner of the mouth. "It's not the lips so much but the small depression that should be right there."

What now? Lunging for the photo, she analyzed the corner of the CEO's mouth. Dammit. Right there. Well, not *right* there. The dimple was so slight it couldn't even be called a dimple. Her issue hadn't been the lips at all, but the mouth in general. And, oh, she could rail about how David had tricked her, about how she specifically meant the lips and the deal would be negated.

But she should have caught that. Even the tiniest of details, as they'd both just learned, could ruin a project.

"David Hennings, I don't know whether to kill you or kiss you."

His hand shot up. "Can I vote?"

She cracked up. "No. But darn it, I can't believe I didn't catch that."

"You were looking too hard. Happens to me sometimes when I'm working cases. I'll be searching for precedents and—bam—someone else reads my notes and in five minutes knows exactly what I need. It's irritating as hell."

"It sure is."

"That being said..."

He strode back to where they'd been sitting, his smile growing wider by the second. *So smug.*

And she'd just handed him that victory.

He slid his phone from the side pocket of his jacket and held it up for her to see. "What time shall I tell the detective we'll be there?"

DETECTIVE LARRY MCCALL ushered Amanda and David into a small conference room at Area North headquarters. The old building didn't have the charm her building had, but with a few fixes and a splash of fresh paint the dreary and dull white walls wouldn't feel so confining. Then again, Amanda supposed a police station wasn't meant to be paradise.

Inside the room, a veneer table large enough for six had been jammed into the corner. Probably the only way it would fit. Five chairs—what happened to the sixth?—were haphazardly pushed in, a couple almost sideways. Maybe the last meeting had ended in a rush.

Amanda took the chair Detective McCall held for her while David remained standing, casually leaning against the wall directly across from her. "Thank you," she said.

"No," the detective said. "Thank you for coming in."

"Detective, please, let's not get ahead of ourselves. As I said—"

McCall waved her off. "Yeah, I know. You're not a forensic artist and you're only having a look. I get it. Still, I appreciate whatever you can do."

He slapped a file onto the table, the *fwap* reverberating in her head, making her ears ring. *What am I doing?* She shouldn't be here. She'd spent years running from the lure of this kind of work. Years. And for good reason. As talented as her mother had been, her work with law enforcement had been the end of the fairy tale. For Amanda. For her father. And most of all, for her mother.

David shifted, drawing her attention, and she brought her gaze to his. He cocked his head—he did that a lot—and stared at her face while she worked on arranging her features into neutral. *No clues here.* Still, he narrowed his eyes and she knew he'd sensed something. Those haunting dark blue eyes of his burned right through her.

The file McCall had slapped on the table was open in front of her and she pulled her gaze from David, needing to be free of whatever psychoanalysis he performed on her. In front of her was a two-dimensional facial reconstruction—a detailed sketch—of a woman with shoulder-length dark hair flipped up at the ends. Big eyes. *So young.* The woman appeared to be late teens, perhaps early twenties. If so, the hair was wrong. No teenager would wear her hair in that style.

Not my call.

Keeping her hands in her lap, Amanda leaned forward. The drawing had been done on bristol paper, its surface rough and able to tolerate abundant erasures.

She glanced at McCall. "Was this done from the skull itself?"

"Uh, no." He reached over, shuffled through some pages in the file and pulled out photos of the skull. "These. Why?"

"Photos can distort the skull. If the lighting is wrong, the artist can misinterpret something."

Which could have been her problem with the photo of the firefighter.

"No foolin'?"

Amanda sat back, still refusing to touch the pages. If she did, they'd somehow bond her. "It can happen. The hair is long. Was there hair found near the skull?"

"Yeah. A few strands. We have it in evidence."

Okay. Well, she knew that was right at least. But truly, if they wanted an accurate image, the artist should have been given access to the skull.

"Did you have any hits at all on the drawing?"

"Not a one."

David finally moved from his spot against the wall and looked over her shoulder at the photo. His presence behind her, looming and steady, sent her body mixed messages. Messages that made her think he could handle anything. That the sheer size of him wouldn't relent. Ever.

Her gaze still on the composite, Amanda cleared her throat. "No missing-person reports?"

"Nothing that fits the timeline. Or her age."

"I'm assuming an anthropologist has studied the bones and given an age estimation?"

"Yeah. His notes are in there. He thinks she was early twenties. White."

Amanda dug through the stack of papers, located the anthropologist's notes and began her review, alternately checking the photos of the skull until she'd read the entire report.

David moved back to his spot against the wall, this time crossing his legs at the ankles and sliding his hands into the front pockets of his jeans. "What do you think?"

"About?"

He shrugged. "Anything. The photo, the file."

"The drawing is good. At least from what I can tell. One thing that's bothering me is that the artist didn't have a chance to study the skull. If I'd been assigned this, I would have requested to see the actual skull."

"What would that have done?"

"Sometimes photography distorts images. As I mentioned, the lighting could throw something off. Plus, I'd want to check tissue-depth data and get a frontal and lateral view of the actual skull. Looking at these photos, it's hard to tell how big it is. All of that plays in to the drawing."

And might be why they didn't get any hits on this poor woman. The artist, although quite good, could have missed something simply because he—or she—was not given the actual skull to sketch from. This victim was buried in a field, tossed away like trash, and the drawing might not even be accurate.

Which meant a family somewhere was still wondering where their loved one could be. And that old yearning for her mother kicked in.

At least she knew where her mother was.

She glanced at the drawing again, and McCall jumped all over her. "What if I could get you the skull? I cleared you with the brass already. They're on board with any help you can offer."

Oh, no. She stacked the papers, setting the anthropologist's report on top of the drawing and the photos of the skull so she didn't have to see them. Didn't have to feel the pull of a dead woman begging for justice.

She bit her bottom lip, really digging in because—*what am I doing?*—as hard as she tried to bury the image of that young woman, it was there, flashing in her mind.

"Amanda?"

David's voice. He was still leaning against the wall, once again studying her, trying to read her. Such a lawyer. Damn him for bringing her here. And damn her for allowing him to do it. For making that stupid bet.

She shoved the folder toward Detective McCall. "If I can see the skull itself, I'll do another drawing so you can compare it to what the other artist did. Having the actual skull might make a difference. That's as far as I'll go, Detective."

McCall bobbed his head, smiling as if he'd won the lottery. "No problem. I'll call the lab, tell 'em you'll be over. Anything you can do is great. We—uh—can't pay you, though. You know that, right?"

Now she looked back at David, grinning at him, returning the smugness he'd hit her with earlier. "Detective, it's your lucky day because Mr. Hennings has agreed to pay my fee. So, as soon as you arrange for me to see that skull, I'll get to work and hopefully, we'll find out where this woman belongs."

WANTING TO BE done with the entire situation, Amanda had agreed to go right over to the lab. Like Pamela Hennings, the detective was on a mission. Which meant David had had to drive her home to pick up her tools.

She'd offered to make the trip to the lab herself, but he'd claimed the least he could do was take her and then pick her up again when she'd completed her work.

Considering her nerves and angst over seeing the skull, Amanda didn't argue. Getting behind a wheel while distracted would do her no good.

And here they were. The forensic anthropologist, Paul something—she'd missed his last name thanks to the ringing in her ears—from the county's forensic lab set the skull with its vacant eyes staring straight up at her on the cork ring. She clasped her fingers together, squeezing hard enough that her knuckles protested, and snapped her mind back to her task rather than her nerves.

Dull beige walls and glaring overhead lights added to the sterile, stark atmosphere of the lab and sent a fierce chill snaking from her feet right up into her torso.

She forced her thoughts to the gloved hands positioning the skull inside the ring. Paul tilted it up another half inch so it would rest against the back of the ring, his hands gentle—reverent even—as he completed his task. This person, whose only remains were the skull in front of them, belonged somewhere.

Give her a name. Whether Amanda could complete that task would be determined, and she'd resist pressuring herself. For now, she'd be an artist, studying a subject, keeping her emotional distance, but doing her best to re-create a drawing that might help identify the victim.

Amanda squeezed the pencil in her hand, then relaxed her grip before she broke the thing. "Tell me about her."

"She's in remarkably good shape considering the elements. Based on the teeth and shape of the head, we're estimating her age at early twenties. Maybe late teens. We made a cast of the skull in case of reconstruction, but there's never been one done. Budgeting issues."

"So the cast is already made?"

Ugh. Amanda closed her eyes, thought of her mother and let out a frustrated laugh. It would be so like her mom to throw this project in her path, urging her to press on because, yes, they had a cast already made and she could take possession of it. To at least try the reconstruction. *Nice, Mom.*

"Yes," Paul said. "It's been sitting here waiting for someone to work on her."

Amanda brought her attention back to the skull on the

table. Detective McCall had told her the anthropologist had determined the victim was a white female, and the flatness of the face and the long, thin nasal openings appeared to represent that.

"She's a Caucasoid," Amanda said.

"Yes." He pointed to an area at the back of the skull. "In terms of injuries, there's a small, depressed spot here. Looks like she was hit with something small, but it was a forceful impact. From the shape of the wound, it could have been a hammer. It fractured her skull."

"Poor thing."

"Whoever buried her didn't dig far enough. That's why the dog dug up the skull. We never found the rest of the bones. Animals may have gotten to them and dragged them to another spot. That field is too big to dig up the entire thing looking for her." He held his hand out. "This is what we have."

Amanda's stomach twisted. "If they'd buried her deeper, she might never have been found."

"Probably not."

"I'll do another sketch. See if it's any different than the last one. I brought everything I need." She pointed her pencil at the table. "Can I work here?"

"That's fine. Holler if you need me."

"I will. Thanks."

Paul wandered off to a lab table with a giant microscope on the far side of the room. From the looks of all the equipment stacked on shelves and the shiny tables, he had plenty to do.

She dug her iPod from her purse, shoved the earbuds in place and scrolled her music library. For this, she knew exactly what she needed. A nice classical mix. She poked at the desired playlist, aptly named DESPERATE, and got down to business.

From her briefcase, she pulled a small stack of tracing paper, pencils and her copy of the tissue-depth table for Caucasoids. In the file Paul had left her, she located the life-size frontal and lateral photographs of the skull, set them side by side on her drawing boards and taped the corners. Over the frontal photograph, she placed tracing paper and began outlining the face while Chopin's Nocturne No. 2 softly streamed through her earbuds.

Song after song played as she carefully outlined, corrected and outlined again, taking her time, double-checking each element until it was time to call Paul over to help with tissue-depth markers. Then she'd begin filling in the face, adding the contours of the jaw and cheeks and then the eyebrows and hairline. The tiny details she could add later, but for now she focused on a blueprint to work with. Little by little, each element brought some new aspect to the face, giving it lifelike qualities.

The hair. Detective McCall had told her they'd found a few long, dark hairs with the body. How long, she wasn't sure, but she'd try shoulder length. After outlining the overall shape of the hair and filling in the length based on the hair found at the scene, she added subshapes—loose waves in the front—and then blended dark and light tones for contrast.

Chopin shifted to Beethoven again. Could that be? More than two hours' worth of a playlist? And she still had to fill in the details on the frontal eye–nose area. She stopped shading and glanced around. Paul had moved to a desk in the corner of the lab, clearly unconcerned about the approaching end of the workday.

Amanda sat back and stretched her shoulders as a beautiful young woman with sharp cheekbones and a small button nose stared back at her.

A woman with a hole in the back of her skull.

Stomach knotted, Amanda closed her eyes, forcing herself to detach. To not get sucked into the mind-ravaging warfare this case would create. Her mother had done this work on a regular basis, felt this pull of longing and heartbreak. Amanda supposed a person eventually got used to it. After all, the cause was noble, if not emotionally eviscerating.

She opened her eyes to someone whose family had yet to know her fate. Amanda thought back to those first brutal days without her mom, to the shock and anger and bone-shattering ache that came with sudden and tragic loss.

To this day, she didn't fully understand—probably never would—how her mom had thought suicide was the only option. Obviously, the emotional place her mother had reached was too dark, too painful to find her way free. Her work as a forensic artist probably hadn't helped, but Amanda would never truly know why her mom had done what she did.

At least Amanda had a place to visit. A place to sit and talk and grieve.

A proper grave site.

She ran her fingertips over the edge of the paper she'd sketched on. This woman's family had no answers. Maybe they assumed she was dead. Maybe not. Maybe down deep they held on to hope that she'd walk back into their lives.

And that tore into Amanda like a rusty chain saw. At least she knew her mother was gone.

"I'll bring you home," she said.

Chapter Four

While David stood beside her at the lab table, Amanda stored her drawing boards, wondering what kind of coward buried a woman and walked away, leaving her body to be ravaged by animals and the elements.

She didn't know. Didn't care to. All she knew was sitting in that lab, staring at the skull, sketching based on estimations of tissue depth, she'd experienced a buzz, the high of having the ability to change the course of an investigation—something her mother used to talk about. Amanda had never experienced it. Never quite understood the lure of forensic work. As a kid, she'd thought it all seemed…morbid…and she hadn't grasped what her mother found so intriguing.

Until today.

She thought about her workbench back in the studio where a forensic workshop registration—the one she kept putting off—was weighted down by a giant conch shell she'd found on a trip to Florida when she was nine. A shell her mother had uncovered while wading in the surf.

I know, Mom. I know. Every day she'd been without her mother, she'd never doubted her presence.

Beside her, David stepped closer and she glanced up, their gazes locking because when he pinned those haunting dark blue eyes on her, she couldn't resist the pull of them reaching right in and paralyzing her.

Something she didn't want to feel. With anyone.

"Everything okay?"

"Fine."

Breaking eye contact, she studied the intricate stitching on the shoulder of his jacket and the way the seam fell at exactly the right spot, the cut so perfect for his big body that she realized it might be nice, sometime soon, to have sex.

And wow. What a mess her mind was today. She couldn't deny there was a certain heat between them. From the time she'd opened her front door, she'd felt it. That simmer.

"This project," she said, keeping her voice low so she wouldn't be overheard by Paul, who patiently waited for them to get packed up. "It's complicated."

Receiving her message that she didn't want Paul eavesdropping, David dipped his head lower. "The sketching?"

No. *You.* "It's more than that."

Because with him she felt things, tingly things that made her system hum, gave her a little high. If only she liked that high. Highs and lows, in her experience, shattered lives. But it had been so long since she was beyond her personal safe zone. Since she allowed herself to immediately feel a certain way about a man. About this man. Feelings like that messed with her emotions, brought her to places that terrified her. For ten years she'd worked to not turn into a person tortured by her own emotions.

But David kept surprising her. In a good way. In a way that made something warm and gooey chase away the cold, empty heartbreak she'd felt in the lab. That alone was worth…she didn't know. She'd simply never met anyone who affected her this way. And so quickly.

Needing to get her mind right, she shook her head and stored her iPod in her bag while the quiet in the lab made her arms itch. Too quiet.

"When I was nine," she said, "my mom found a conch shell on the beach in Florida. I have it on my workbench where I can see it every day. It's a paperweight for important things. Right now one of those things is a registration form for a forensic workshop I've been thinking about taking. Pretty high-level stuff. I keep putting off registering."

"Why?"

She gave up on packing her things and faced him. "My mother was a forensic artist."

His eyebrows lifted. "She doesn't do it anymore?"

"She died. Ten years ago. Killed herself."

Wow, Amanda. Totally on a roll here. That miserable fact had only been spoken a handful of times and each time to people who'd proved their loyalty. People she could trust. Apparently, David was now one of those people.

"I can't imagine that. I'm sorry." He stood, unmoving, his face completely neutral, no judgment or horror, just a mild curiosity over whether she'd continue.

"Thank you. But I'm only telling you so you understand. She did a drawing once that helped convict a man of murder. He went to prison for a few years and was later exonerated. She never forgave herself."

His head snapped back and Amanda held up her hand. "She didn't kill herself over it, but it didn't help. My mother always battled depression. She may have been bipolar. I'm not sure. All I know is that there were tremendous highs followed by days she couldn't get out of bed. Work was her savior. She loved making a difference. After that man was exonerated she never did another sketch. Never. I think the loss of her work sent her into a spiral she couldn't come out of."

"And now we're asking you to do a reconstruction."

"Yes."

David cracked his neck, finally showing some indication of his thoughts. "If I'd known, I wouldn't have pressured you."

"I'll do the sculpture," she said.

For a moment he stood in his spot, his face deadpan, not even a flinch as dead air clogged the space between them. "I'm… Wow. What made you change your mind?"

So many things. *My mother. An unidentified dead woman.* She pointed at the image she'd created still sitting on the lab table. "Look at her. She was a beautiful girl. At least from my interpretation."

He reached for the sketch, then stopped, his hand in midair. "May I?"

"Sure."

"Your work is amazing."

He set the image back on the table and angled back to her. "Are you okay?"

"I am. I thought doing the work my mother loved would be this big dramatic scene where I'd be doomed by my own emotional sludge. Turns out, it wasn't so bad. If anything, I got a taste of what my mom went through each time. It's odd, but it was like I had a piece of her right there with me, and that made me come alive a little bit." Oh, what a thing to say to a man she barely knew. "I'm just babbling."

"You're not. I get it." He winced. "Ew. Sorry. No, I don't get it. Not really. What I should have said was I can see where, in a weird way, you'd connect with the work."

All she could do was nod. Talking about this, letting

him dissect her and examine her motivations, wouldn't help her stay detached.

From the work or him.

"If they'll give me the cast of the skull, I'll try it. The reconstruction will be 3-D and have much more detail than my sketch."

Appropriate or not, and definitely not caring that Paul sat just across the room, she stepped closer, slid her hand under David's jacket around his waist and went up on tiptoes to hug him. "Thank you for being a pushy Hennings. After spending the afternoon in the lab, I believe my mother is letting me know it's time I use my talent for more than what I've been doing."

He backed away from the hug and hit her with one of his amazing smiles, not lightning quick but a slow-moving and devastating one that creeped across his face and kicked off a tingle low in her belly.

"Well, we Hennings people like to do our civic duty. How about as a thank you for saving me from my mother's wrath, I buy you dinner one night this week? I can't do it tonight because I'm expected at my mother's."

"You don't have to feed me."

"Yeah, I do. You're doing this for us despite what you've been through. Besides, what I really want is a date with you, so a dinner kills two birds with one stone. As they say."

So slick, this one. Total charmer. And such trouble. But trouble, right now, might be nice. "I think I'd like that."

"JUST PULL UP in front and drop me off," Amanda said as David turned the corner leading to her building.

He double-parked and turned off the engine. "I'll walk you to the door."

"David—"

But he'd already hopped out to get the door for her, which, the girlie-girl buried deep inside admitted, gave her a little thrill.

The door flew open and he waved her out, adding a little bow that made her laugh. How she loved a man who could make her laugh.

"Do you need help getting upstairs?"

"No." She retrieved her briefcase and tote from the backseat. "I'm all set. Thank you, though."

"I'll walk you to the door."

Early-evening darkness had fallen and the streetlamps gave her building a creepy glow. Having been gone all day, she'd neglected to leave any interior lights on. As she approached, she spotted something white stuck to the front door of the building. Vendors were constantly leaving bagged flyers hanging on the door handle, but no one had ever fixed anything to the door. The nerve.

Using the flashlight on her phone, she read the notice—what the heck?—marked City of Chicago, Building Department. Below the letterhead in thick, bold letters the sign left no doubt of the city's request. OFF-LIMITS. DO NOT ENTER.

She tilted her head, pondering this not-so-minor development. It had to be a joke. She glanced back at David a few steps behind her, thinking maybe he'd have… Nah. He hardly knew her well enough to pull this kind of prank. One she wouldn't think funny.

At all.

"What's up?" David asked. "Did you forget something?"

"I…" Stumped, she held her hand to the door. "I don't know. There's a sign from the city telling me not to enter."

Has to be a joke. Right? Because if it wasn't, she had big problems. But why would her building be sealed?

Something odd squeezed her stomach, shooting tension right into her chest. Without access to the building, she'd be locked out of her studio and home. Out of her life.

Frowning, David looked up at the door. "Why?"

As if she knew. She shone the flashlight on the paragraph below the big block letters and scanned it while the pressure in her head skyrocketed and a sharp throb settled behind her eyes. "It says the building must remain vacant until further notice. Are they *kidding* me? My entire life is in this building."

"They must have the wrong location. Plus, they haven't barricaded or padlocked the door."

"What does that mean?"

"It means the building isn't going to collapse. If it was they'd block the entrances. The city can't afford to barricade every door and window on every building. If the problem is due to contaminants and the building won't collapse, they do signage. Which they've done, so don't panic. Call your landlord and find out what's happening."

Yes. The landlord. The city had to have contacted him. Quickly, she scrolled through her contacts and found the number. "I've been trying to convince him to apply for landmark status on this building. And they want to *condemn* it?"

The phone rang a third time and Amanda grunted. "He never answers when I call." She left a voice mail explaining the situation, then disconnected. "I'm calling the building department."

"You can try, but it's after five. They're probably gone for the day."

She'd try anyway. Couldn't hurt. Not wanting to deal with searching for the number on her phone, she dialed information and was connected to the city's building department, where—yes—she received a recorded message telling her the office was indeed closed.

Terrific. She tapped the screen and scrunched her eyes closed. *Stay calm. Just a mix-up.*

Opening her eyes, she once again read the sign as her thoughts raced. *Work. Clothes. Checkbook.* Her damned allergy medicine. Everything was inside.

Forget calm.

Forget not panicking.

All at once, her body buzzed and throbbed and itched and all this emotional garbage was so not good for her, the woman who kept her life in a constant state of neither ups nor downs. Well, this was one heck of a down. "I don't know what to do. My clothes are all in there!" She flapped her arms. "My *work* is in there."

"Hang tight." David retreated a few steps and stared up at the darkened building, obviously formulating some kind of plan. "There's a back door, right?"

"Yes."

"We're going in the back."

"The sign says…"

"Yeah, but you just said you don't have any clothes. We'll sneak in the back door, hope we don't get caught and you pack up whatever you need for a few days until this gets hashed out."

Without the studio, she couldn't work. Without work, she couldn't earn. Her draining checkbook—the one inside the no-access building—filled her mind. "I lease a storage unit, but there's not enough room for me to work in there. I have a sculpture to finish!"

David slid the tote and her briefcase off her shoulders, walked back to his SUV and stowed them. "I've got this. My condo is still being renovated. You can use one of the bedrooms that's not being worked on. I'll put you in the guest room."

Amanda's head dipped forward. "You're letting me turn your condo into a studio?"

"Why not? The place is empty. You might as well use it until I can move in." He waved his hand at the building. "This'll get straightened out in a few days and you can move back here. No problem." He inched closer and grabbed both her hands. "We've got this. We'll load as much as we can and take it over to the condo."

The idea might not be a bad one. It might, in fact, be a short-term solution. "We can use my car also."

"Good. Then we'll get you set up in a hotel for the night. Is that a plan?"

"David Hennings, I could love you."

He threw his hands up, grinning at her. "Let's not get crazy now or you might be stuck with me."

At the moment, as she thought about every minute she'd spent with this man since he'd walked into her studio earlier that day, being stuck with him might not be a bad thing. She grabbed hold of his jacket, the leather Belstaff she loved so much, and dragged him closer. Going up on tiptoes, she kissed him. And it wasn't one those tentative let's-test-this kisses where they sort of eased into it. This one left nothing on the table. Tongues were involved.

And *she'd* started it. Total insanity.

But he certainly wasn't rejecting her. He made it worth her while by wrapping his arm around her and pulling her right up against him. A few seconds later a bulge at his crotch area announced itself in a truly obvious way, and her heart slammed. What he wanted couldn't have been clearer. No doubt. At all.

"Dude," a guy passing by said. "Lucky dog."

David pulled back and his amazing lips tilted into a wicked grin. "Dude," he said, "don't I know it?"

DAVID SET THE last box of supplies they'd taken from Amanda's in his extra bedroom and did a quick survey of the place. The walls were still unpainted and the drywall dust left a weird coating on the floors. For what she needed, it would do. If the dust didn't give her an asthma attack. "We'll run out tonight and get you a couple of tables to set up. It won't be perfect, but this is triage."

"Yes. Triage. I'm hoping whatever the mix-up is will be taken care of tomorrow and I can move back home."

Having dealt with bureaucratic red tape, David wasn't feeling hopeful. Miracles could happen, he supposed.

She checked her watch. "It's only six. I can still hit the office supply store for the tables. You said you have dinner at your mom's tonight. Go. You don't have to do this with me."

Whatever he expected her to say, that wasn't it. And yeah, part of him was insulted that she thought he'd leave her to handle this mess on her own. He propped his hands on his hips and shook his head. "My mother raised me better than that. We'll go get the tables and then I'll head out. I'll still be on time."

If he did ninety on the Eisenhower and didn't shower before dinner.

"Whoa," she said. "Don't be mad. Please."

"I'm not mad." He held up a hand. "Wait. Yeah. Maybe I am. I don't know what kind of men you've had in your life, but I'm not about to leave you alone with this."

"I'm sorry. I didn't mean..." She closed her eyes, shook her head. "I'm sorry. I'm not used to the help. I just don't want to be a problem."

"You're not. Let's get you tables. On the way, I'll make

some calls. See if any of my contacts know anyone in the city's building department. If that doesn't work, I'll pull out the big guns."

"The big guns?"

"My mother."

Amanda laughed. At least something made her laugh.

"Don't laugh. Do you know how many people in this town owe my mother a favor? She's sat on the board of every major charity. The mayor takes her calls on a regular basis. Favors don't come cheap, though. She'll help us, but if she does, she'll owe someone and I don't like putting her in that position. I could also ask my sister for help. She'll *love* that."

Wait, had he *ever* asked Penny for help? Most likely he hadn't. It would have become a weapon between them. The fact that their relationship had reached that point didn't say anything good about either of them.

"Why?"

"We…uh…don't get along. We're basically oil and water."

Because of the lack of chairs, Amanda leaned against the wall. "She must have had a hand in it."

"We should be ashamed of ourselves."

"You're siblings. There's bound to be some infighting."

"What about you? Brothers or sisters?"

"Two stepbrothers," she said. "My dad remarried five years ago."

"Was that hard?"

She scooped her water bottle from her giant purse and swigged. "No. And I wonder about that. Shouldn't it have been rough for me to see my father happy with someone else?"

"From what you've said—and I mean no disrespect

here—life with your mom wasn't easy. You know it, and your dad would definitely have known it. What's wrong with wanting someone you love to be happy?"

"I guess. In the beginning I was afraid it meant something. That somehow I was wrong for wanting my father to have a quiet—and stable—life."

"I'll tell ya, you worry a lot."

"I do. I'm always thinking. It's maddening."

He wandered over to her. "I can help with that."

She rolled her eyes but laughed. God, he loved to make her laugh. It was like every exceptional thing that had ever happened to him in one giant sound.

"I'm serious," he said. "I think a lot, too, but not like you. I don't worry like you do. It's gonna be what it's gonna be. Me worrying about it won't help. It's paying interest on a debt I don't owe. Who needs that?"

She cocked her head. Considered that. "That's a good way to think about it. Thank you."

"Amanda LeBlanc, you need fun in your life."

"I have fun in my life."

"Not my kind of fun. The kind of fun that has you on the back of a motorcycle tearing down country roads. Girl, you need to let go once in a while. Preferably with me."

"Promises, promises."

"Just take a chance. You'll see." He tugged on the end of her hair. "Now we need to go before I'm late for dinner and my mother murders me."

Chapter Five

Some things in life were out of David's control. Rainy days, crabby clients, the plague.

Family dinners.

He paused at the base of the stairs and listened to the chatter coming from the dining room. *The gang's all here.* Of course, he was late.

Blame it on his mother, who'd hooked him into this cold-case business. Even though Amanda LeBlanc had turned out to be beautiful—and alluring, smart, talented and *sexy* as hell—he'd still spent the better part of his day working on his mom's project.

"Where's *David*?" he heard Penny ask from the other room.

His sister had a snarky tone that hit his ears like nails fired from a gun and he bit down, already trying to control his rising temper. *Breathe, dude.* He inhaled, held his breath for a few seconds and then slowly let it out.

"Upstairs," Zac said. "He walked in with us. He's getting cleaned up."

"He's late for dinner and he didn't even need to drive anywhere?"

Holy hell, his sister made him nuts. From the time she was seven years old and wrapping everyone around her finger, getting him and Zac in trouble all the time, he'd learned to accept her power over this family. But sometimes it ate him raw. Time to break this up. He swung around the staircase and marched into the dining room, where his dad was just landing in his normal spot at the head of the table. His mom would sit at the opposite end by the windows, and David would sit to her right. From there, he wasn't sure. With Zac and Penny having significant others now, the seating arrangements could have changed. Another reminder of how long he'd been away. Penny stood at the sideboard pouring a glass of wine and Russ stood next to her.

"I'm right here," David said. "Sorry I'm late."

"Hey," Zac said, holding a chair for Emma, who looked pretty in one of those wrap dresses that were suddenly back in style. "No prob. I told them you were late getting back."

David looked over at Penny, who had her big blue eyes pinned to him. "I heard," he said.

"Oh, puh-lease. All I said was you were late and didn't have to drive anywhere. That's it."

She jammed the stopper on the wine decanter with enough force the thing should have splintered. But, as usual, no one said anything about the dramatics.

He'd be the bigger person and not take the Penny bait. Regardless of whose fault it was, their every argument started this way. One of them said something that, on the surface, seemed harmless but underneath held enough venom to kill an elephant. He wasn't going there. He'd promised Mom—and himself—he'd find a way to mend things with his sister.

He walked over and shook hands with Penny's boyfriend. "Russ, good to see you."

"Hey, Dave."

The FBI agent, still in his suit from work, his dark

hair neatly groomed, stayed cool. He'd been that way the first time they'd met in person the week prior. Not surprising, considering that Penny had probably filled him in on their constant arguing. It didn't matter. As he should be, Russ was Team Penny, and David respected that. Loyalty in a relationship, at least in David's mind, could make or break things.

He turned to Penny and touched her arm. "I don't want to fight with you."

Hitting him with direct suspicion, she narrowed those piercing blue eyes, but he stayed quiet, refusing to start a war.

Finally, she nodded. "Me, neither. Mom is really excited about this dinner. Let's not ruin it."

"A truce," Russ said. "Someone alert the media."

Zac took his seat next to Emma. "Nice."

Russ laughed. "You think I'm kidding?"

Penny flapped her hands. "Okay, *Russell*. Knock it off."

Waiting to see where Penny and Russ would land, David stood behind his chair. Russ moved to the opposite side, next to Emma and facing Penny. That meant David would be in his normal spot by Mom with Penny on his opposite side.

"Hey, Dad," he said.

"Son, how was your day?"

Ha. That was a loaded question. "Busy."

The table was packed with food, his favorite roast, a ham—because apparently the roast wasn't enough—a huge dish of twice-baked potatoes, salad and some kind of vegetable dish. Never a fan of vegetables, he'd try it, but chances were it wouldn't work for him. The aroma of the meat mixed with spices from the vegetables, and his stomach rumbled. No lunch. He'd forgotten. What with the hotness of Amanda LeBlanc distracting him.

He took his seat and dropped his napkin into his lap.

"Hellooo, my darlings." Mom swung into the room, her hair tucked behind her ears and a fresh face of makeup. "How are we all tonight?"

A variety of responses sounded as his mother worked her way around the table, bending low to kiss each of them on the cheek. At least until she got to David, who was still dressed, as she'd put it that morning, like a prison escapee.

It wouldn't make her happy, but he'd already gotten home late, and another fifteen minutes to shower and change would have thrown off her carefully crafted schedule.

"Oh, David," his mother said. "Really?"

Dad held his hands up. "Already? What is it?"

"She's mad I'm wearing jeans."

Mom smacked his shoulder and moved to her seat. "I'm not *mad*."

"Yeah, you are. And I'm sorry. I was running around working on your project all afternoon. My choice was to shower, change and let the food get cold or just wash up quick. I chose to not ruin your meal."

"You were doomed either way," Zac said.

"Amen, brother."

Penny passed the dinner rolls without snagging one. "What project?"

"Well," Mom said, "I hope it's good news."

David took two rolls and passed the basket to Mom. "Eh. Halfway. I got her to talk to the detective. She spent all afternoon working on a new drawing. You're going to owe her big for that alone, but she's agreed to do your reconstruction. And, oh yeah, while she was at the lab viewing the skull, the building she lives and works out of got condemned."

Clothing issue already forgotten, Mom's jaw dropped. *"Condemned?"*

"It has to be a mistake. The place, for as old as it is, is in great shape. Anyway, I set her up in my condo so she has a place to work. She's staying in a hotel until it gets sorted out."

"What project?" Penny repeated.

Mom passed the basket of rolls on. "David is helping me on another cold case."

From the other end of the table, Dad coughed up whatever he was drinking. Russ shot out of his chair and slapped Dad's back a few times.

"Are you all right, dear?" Mom asked, perfectly calm, and David had to laugh.

Dad didn't look all right. Not with the red cheeks that probably had nothing to do with the coughing fit. "I'm fine. Is this the cold case you and Irene eavesdropped on last night? You're not volunteering us again, are you?"

"No. Of course not. I spoke to Irene this morning. They're willing to help. So David is handling it this time."

What now? David stabbed his fork into a couple of slices of roast and then grabbed some ham. "Uh, no, I'm not. I told you I'd do this one thing. That's it. From here on out it's someone else's deal. I'm not an investigator and I'm damned sure not a criminal attorney."

The minute—no, second, *milli*second—it left his mouth, he regretted it. Replaying it in his mind, he knew it sounded bad. As if he was once again singling himself out from his family. Penny had never been one to let that go. And then Dad and Zac would take her side and Mom would try to stay neutral, but that never worked because staying neutral meant she wasn't on either side. Which made David the one standing alone, irritated and feeling childish.

But he'd nix it straight away. "I didn't mean—"

"Yes, *David*," Penny drawled, "we're aware that you chose civil law. What's the matter? Bored? Coming to the dark side?"

"Penny," Russ said, his voice tinged with warning.

David breathed in and held his hand up. "It's okay. That sounded bad. I was about to say I didn't mean it the way it sounded."

Penny sawed at the roast on her plate. "Well, that'd be a first, wouldn't it?"

So much for the truce. His plan for making nice with his sister had been an epic fail. But this was years of damage done by the two of them and he'd take his share of the responsibility. He'd had his own demons to battle—petty jealousy, for one. Penny was not only the baby, but also the only girl, so she basically got away with murder. She'd also become the golden child their father could groom into taking over the firm. A role David had rejected and shouldn't have been bothered by, but he'd allowed it to intensify his resentment of his sister. At least until recently when he'd realized it wasn't Penny's role at the firm he envied, but their father's approval.

And now it needed to stop.

David stood, tossed his napkin onto the table and tugged his sister's jacket sleeve. "Come with me."

"No."

"We need to talk."

"I'm eating."

"I know. We need to talk. Now."

"No, David. I'm hungry and this food will get cold."

Russ jerked his head sideways. "Penny."

Points to him for trying to get his girlfriend to cooperate.

"Whatever it is, David, we can talk here."

Great. She wanted to do it in front of everyone. Whatever. "Fine. We'll talk here. I'm home now. Okay? Moved all the way back here from Boston because guess what? It would be nice to feel like a part of this family."

"And whose fault—"

"My fault. But you helped me out the door. I'll own my part, but you're not exactly easy. Now, though? I'm tired of fighting. I want my sister back. But you, you're like a…a panther…ready to pounce on every damned thing I say and it wears me the hell out. Every time we're together I have to mentally psyche myself up for it. Let's forget the stupidity and figure out how to get along."

Any chatter going on stopped. Zac sighed, grabbed a roll out of the basket in front of him, tore it in two and handed half to Emma. "Eat. You'll need your strength."

And Emma, God bless her, laughed.

Apparently horrified over her outburst, she slapped her hand over her mouth, forgetting, of course, about the roll, and wound up bouncing it off her nose.

Everyone, including David, cracked up. Who knew sweet, levelheaded Emma had comedic timing?

"Mrs. Hennings," she said, "I'm so sorry."

But Mom laughed right along with them. "Oh, Emma, not at all. Thank you for the diversion." She swung her finger between David and Penny. "Please compromise. David, let her eat and then the two of you can go in the study and work this out. Kill each other if you must, but do not ruin my meal."

"Wow, Mom," Zac said.

"You." She poked her finger at him. "Hush."

David took his seat again, flattened his napkin in his

lap and started shoveling food because Emma wasn't the only one who'd need strength.

"Can we talk about this cold case?" Dad asked. "Is it that skull you told me about last night?"

Mom set her fork down and sat back in her chair. "Yes. The skull. You said your investigators were busy and David is bored. He agreed to do it."

Swallowing the mound of food in his mouth, David turned to his father. "Now, *that's* funny. I told her I'd talk to the sculptor. That's all."

His mother. Unbelievable. David slammed the full glass of water in front of him. As soon as dessert was cleared and he had his chat with Penny, he was going to bed. Crazy, exhausting day.

Penny gripped his sleeve and he glanced down. Still hanging on, she leaned over. "I'm sorry. I don't want to fight anymore, either. I'll try. I promise."

"Thank you. By the way—" he leaned closer, bumping her shoulder "—I love you. I haven't said that enough. You drive me nuts, but I do love you."

"Huh. You really are full of surprises tonight."

"Penny," Russ said.

But his sister kept her gaze focused on David and smiled up at him. "I love you, too. And I'm glad you're back. Even if you drive me nuts, too."

AT TEN THE next morning, accompanied by Detective McCall and David, Amanda again entered the county forensic lab, but unlike the day before, she knew what to expect from this particular visit. Yesterday, she'd been determined to draw the sketch and be done with her end of this bargain. At least until she'd set eyes on the actual skull. She'd seen human skulls before in classes and workshops, but in those instances, the experience was more clinical. An artist studying a subject. This time, when she looked at the skull, studied the wound on the back of it, she imagined a young woman, someone younger than herself, getting her head bashed.

And that, she almost couldn't stand. Her death had most likely been fast, but no one should suffer the violence surrounding it. Particularly a twenty-year-old woman.

Paul, the forensic anthropologist she'd met yesterday, glanced over, spotted them and set aside some bones he'd been working with. His lips lifted into a small smile. "Good to see you back."

Amanda nodded. "Hi, Paul." She turned to David. "This is David Hennings, and I think you know Detective McCall."

The men exchanged hellos as Paul led them to the metal table Amanda had worked at the day before. On top sat a box with a manila folder next to it. Amanda assumed that would be the required documentation and copies of any pertinent information she would need to sign for.

Detective McCall walked to the opposite side and shuffled through the folder. "It's all here?"

"Far as I know." Paul faced Amanda. "We gave you copies of photos of where the body was found, the detective's notes, the anthropologist's report and the dentist's report. We just need you to sign everything out."

McCall handed one of the sheets over and Amanda perused it. At the very top it read Forensic Art Activity Report and below that was written the name of the law-enforcement division she'd be working with. In this case, Special Crimes. Whatever that meant. Below that were boxes asking for administrative details of the case, the date, who requested the work to be done, the case number and so on. The next larger section pertained to the examination and analysis portion of the investigation. That section requested everything from the race and sex of the victim to the clothing and accessories that may have accompanied the body. Sadly, in this case, Amanda would only be taking the skull cast and copies from the case file.

She read through the file quickly, then glanced at the box where the plaster cast waited for her to take possession. *What am I doing?* Last night she'd been so sure this was the right decision, but once she signed this paperwork she was in it. Knee-deep, which was terrifying. Sure, she could always back out, tell the detective she'd tried but couldn't do it. She wasn't on their payroll and wouldn't be taking taxpayer dollars, but she'd given her word. If she backed out, she'd disappoint all parties.

And commitment meant something.

I'm stuck. She let out a small breath and glanced at the box again. Beside her, David angled toward her and she could feel that penetrating gaze reading her.

"Uh, fellas," he said, "wanna give us a minute?"

Thank you.

After a short pause, McCall nodded. "No problem."

Amanda waited for Paul and the detective to reach the far side of the room where Paul had been working when they'd first arrived.

She set the pen on the table and David puckered his lips slightly before shifting an inch closer and nudging her with his elbow. "Second thoughts?"

"Nerves."

"You're about to take possession of a skull with the intent of reconstructing it and helping identify a murder victim. I'd say feeling nervous is reasonable."

To him maybe. To her it brought every fear, all those years of wondering what her mother's life had been like, the emotional toll, bubbling up. Since her mother's death, she'd fought the negativity, fought the desire to try forensic work, fought the urge to make a difference because somewhere down deep, she knew, it would be all-consuming. The highs and lows that came with this type of work would be constant. All-consuming meant winding up like her mother.

That, she would not do.

"Look," he said, "if you don't want to do this, we'll walk out of here. Personally, I think you're intrigued by this project. You did the sketch hoping that would be enough. Then you saw the sketch and decided to do the reconstruction. At each juncture you've tried to talk yourself out of this. Maybe that's your pattern, this going back and forth. I don't know. Doesn't really matter. But if you leave without that skull, you'll always wonder. And that's a rotten way to live."

She tapped her fingers against the table, considering the options. What if she pulled it off? What if she took this skull back to her studio—well, David's condo, which was her makeshift studio—completed the reconstruction and was able to help them identify the woman?

Really, that should be her only thought right now. Rather than worrying about her own emotional stability, she should focus on the victim. On bringing this woman home and giving her family answers.

She picked up the pen, rolled it between her fingers—*do it*—and scribbled her name on the form. Then she shoved it as far across the table as she could, hoping it would keep her from changing her mind and ripping the thing up.

David laughed. "You're cute, Amanda."

McCall and Paul wandered back over. Paul took possession of the form—*it's done now*—and slid the box in front of her.

"We packed it good to protect it." He tapped the top of the box. "It's only a cast, but she's been here a while. Take good care of her."

Amanda grasped the box, her fingers wrapping around the edges as she slid it toward her. "I will. She'll be safe with me."

Chapter Six

At the condo, David placed the box containing the skull cast on one of the folding tables they'd set up the night before. He wasn't sure where Amanda would want it positioned but figured his best option was to let her deal with it in her own way. Give her some space.

Later.

Right now he'd like to take her to lunch, maybe get her mind off the fact that the city still hadn't returned her landlord's calls.

David had pretty much decided to give the landlord until the end of the day to make something happen. After that, he'd work his own contacts to speed things up.

"I have an idea," he said.

"What's that?"

"I have a buddy. Brian Dyce. His mom was at the fund-raiser you attended the other night."

"She sat at my table. Lovely woman. You're friends with her son?"

"We went to grammar school together. That was before his parents started the youth center and his father became a bigwig. If you have time, I'll take you to lunch now and then we could swing by the center. Show them your sketch. It's a long shot, but they know people at the area shelters. Maybe someone will recognize the woman."

Amanda poked him in the chest. “I like it. Good thinking.”

“Eh. I can’t take all the credit. My mother said she paved the way.”

He cocked his arm out and she glanced down, a slow smile drifting across her face. After that poke to the chest, he didn’t think linking her arm with his would be a hardship. Except waiting for her to respond could be a slow, paralyzing rejection and he couldn’t seem to move his arm.

When she finally grabbed hold, his stomach unclenched enough that he might actually be able to put food in it.

It’d been months—many—since he’d walked arm in arm with a woman. In Boston, he’d kept to himself, dating occasionally but not anyone steady. Mostly, dating was about sex and getting it and he had a knack for finding just the right women. Ones who, like him, wanted a good time and would treat the person well when they were together. All in all, not a bad life. No strings, no responsibilities, no hassles.

Now, with Amanda’s arm tucked in his, it made him think the life he’d left in Boston wasn’t so great. It had worked then. Got him through. Being home, though, seeing his younger sister and brother in relationships and on their way to settling down made him the only one without a significant other at the dinner table, and he wasn’t sure he liked that.

“Phew,” he cracked. “Scared me there.”

“I can’t imagine anything scares you.”

“A lot of things scare me,” he said. “I’m not about to admit them, though.”

“Except your mother.”

He laughed. “Yeah. That one I’ll own. *Everyone* is afraid of her.”

“I like you, David Hennings.”

Good to know. Because he liked her, too.

MRS. DYCE CHARGED into the lobby of the youth center, her conservative heels clicking against the tile and her face lit up like a kid’s at Christmas. She wrapped David in a hug that should have broken his spine. The woman was a good seven inches smaller than him, but she had one hell of a grip.

“It’s so wonderful to see you.” She released him but still held on to his arms. “Have you seen Brian? He stopped over the other night and mentioned he’d called you.”

In the years David had been acquainted with this family, certain things never changed. Mrs. Dyce’s energy for one. Still rail thin, she moved quickly, all the time, and she never said just one thing. It was always a rush of thoughts that flew. Some would call her impulsive, but that, in his opinion, didn’t fit. She had stamina and a brain that operated on rapid-fire 100 percent of the time.

“Yep. Getting together next weekend. We got caught up on the phone, though.”

“Good.”

She stepped back and held her hand to Amanda. “How nice to see you again, Amanda. Welcome. Come back to my office and we’ll talk.”

He gestured Amanda ahead of him and followed her down the long hallway lined with doors on each side. The walls had been painted a sandy beige rather than the stark white they’d been the last time David visited. The beige was better. Warmer. More welcoming.

Ahead of him, Amanda’s head swung back and forth

as she took in the various artwork along the way. Nothing fancy or overdone, but enough to give the corridor some life.

Near the end of the hallway, Mrs. Dyce hung a right into her office and waved them to the guest chairs in front of her desk. She tucked her hair—was it more red than the last time he'd seen her?—behind her ears and took a seat behind the desk. Like his mother, she was high profile in the city and often wound up in the local media. With that came pressure to look a certain way, and Mrs. Dyce took that seriously. She'd definitely had a face-lift recently, because her skin was as smooth as a baby's bottom, and at her age, that just wasn't possible. But she looked healthy and elegant and camera ready.

She closed an open file on her desk and set it aside, giving them her complete attention. "Tell me why you're here." She leveled one of her playful smiles on him. "Other than you missed me dragging you around by your ear."

Amanda slid him a pointed look. Together, these two women would be a handful. Add them to the list of things he feared. He smacked his hands together. "Anyway…"

Mrs. Dyce laughed. "Yes. *Anyway.*"

David held up the large envelope containing extra copies of the sketch. "I think my mom mentioned Amanda is helping the police on a cold case."

"It came up when I spoke to her yesterday. Something about an unidentified skull."

"Yes, ma'am. Amanda has completed a composite image of what the victim might look like. She's also doing a reconstruction."

If Mrs. Dyce's eyebrows could move, they would have, but the overall effect was her eyes widening. "A *recon-*

struction." She drew out the word. "As in you'll re-create the face?"

Amanda nodded. "Yes, ma'am."

"Fascinating. How wonderful."

David pushed one of the copies of the sketch across the table. "This is Amanda's rendering of what the person may have looked like. Do you think you could show it to Mr. Dyce or some of your contacts at the shelters? Maybe someone saw her. It's a long shot, but…"

She kept her eyes on David as she leaned forward to glance at the sketch. "Absolutely. But five years is a long time, David. Thousands of people go through city shelters. I know just from the number of kids I see here every day how hard it is to remember everyone."

"But it's worth a try, right?"

"It's always worth a try. Who knows? With everyone Mr. Dyce knows and my contacts, maybe someone will recognize her." She picked up the sketch and studied it for a minute, and her lips parted slightly. She looked back at Amanda. "You drew this? It's quite good."

"I did. I had the skull to work from. It won't be exact, but I'm hoping it's close. The real details will come when I do the reconstruction. I like to think of the sketch as the blueprint."

"Well, it's an amazing blueprint. I'd love to see some of your work. Maybe we could set something up?"

"I'd like that." She dug in her purse for a card and handed it over. "Call me anytime. I could bring you some things to look at."

"Wonderful."

Seeing as they'd done what they came to do—and even got Amanda a potential client as a bonus—David stood. "We won't keep you."

He held his hand out, helping Amanda from the chair,

and the normalcy of it, the feel of her skin against his—he liked it. So he held on, linking his fingers with hers.

Taking note of the gesture, Mrs. Dyce gave him a wry smile. "Mr. Dyce will be sorry he missed you. He's out at a meeting."

"Tell him congratulations on the presidential appointment. What an honor after all the work you have done."

In Chicago, the Dyce name was known for raising awareness of gang and gun violence. When they organized rallies, thousands flooded the streets to hear Mr. Dyce speak. And now those years of work had made him a household name in Washington and grabbed the attention of the president.

"I will. He's thrilled. And anxious to make a difference not just here, but across the country."

David grinned. "Spoken like a true politician's wife."

"Young man, I can still drag you around by your ear."

He leaned down and pecked her on the cheek. "I know. Forgive me."

"It's good to see you. Don't be a stranger." She waved them out. "Get out of here, you two. Go make a difference."

SITTING IN THE front passenger seat of David's SUV, Amanda studied his condo building, a four-story brick structure that, if she guessed correctly, dated back to the early 1900s. Given David's reaction to the building she lived in—the condemned one—his choice of home came as no surprise. The man had a thing for history and classic architecture. This building's aged brick and avant-garde rounded edges reflected both.

"I love your building," she said. "I didn't get a chance to tell you that last night."

His beautiful mouth with those totally kissable full

lips twisted into a smile. "Thanks. Before I even saw the inside, I wanted to live here. It's a total throwback."

"That's how I felt about my place."

"Speaking of which—"

"No news from my landlord."

David shook his head. "If you don't hear anything by the end of the day, I'll get on it. See if I can scare up any info. For now," he held a key up, "here's my extra key for you. Come and go as you please."

Her fingers brushed his as she wrapped her hand around the dangling key and his sultry dark blue eyes bore right into her, leaving her body tense but a little gooey all at the same time.

Where should she take this?

Easily she could invite him inside and they could pull up a couple of the folding chairs they'd bought the night before and talk. And…um…other things.

She bit her bottom lip and thought about those other things and her cheeks fired.

"Damn, you're gorgeous," he said.

"Thank you. But, so help me, David, if you come inside I won't get any work done."

At that, he laughed. He leaned over and brushed his fingers down the side of her face, slowly moving over the curve of her cheek, along her jaw, to her mouth, where he ran the pad of his thumb over her lips. "If that's meant to scare me off, it's not working."

She dipped her head and rubbed her cheek along his fingertips. "It is your condo. I have no right to tell you when you can be here."

But his being there, with the energy between them, would lead to things. Things she wasn't ready for. The man unnerved her and it felt like too much too soon. No matter what, too much too soon was never good. *Safe zone*. That was where she needed to stay. No highs or lows. Particularly now with her home and studio situation leaving her life in flux.

Now she'd send him on his way. Even if her hormones didn't like it.

"I'm not staying," he said. "In case you were wondering. I have a contractor waiting on me at my office."

She pushed the door open but didn't move. A gust of wind blew her hair into her face and she shoved it back. "Okay."

"Unless you want me to."

"That's the problem."

"What?"

She sighed and rested her head back against the seat. "I really sort of stink at relationships. I like you. There's a vibe that makes me want you close. I'm a girl used to being on her own, so I'm confused by it."

He pulled a face, flopping his lower lip out. "We're getting acquainted. Just let it happen. Why do you have to feel a certain way right now?"

"Because loss isn't easy for me." And once again, diarrhea of the mouth around him. *Loss isn't easy?* Goodness, if that didn't send the man running, she might have to marry him. "I'm…"

He held up his hands. "You're careful. I get it."

"But?"

"If you never took a chance on anyone or anything, what fun is that? Are you going to live your life in neutral?"

Another blast of wind whipped through the open door and she shivered. At the cold and his colossal nerve. "I don't live my life in neutral."

"When was the last time you went on a date?"

"Two weeks ago."

His head dipped forward. "Really?"

Take that, fella. "Yes. I date. I happen to be an attractive woman."

"Believe me, I know. Let me rephrase."

"Says the lawyer."

A fast smile lit his face. "And she's quick on her feet, too. When's the last time you had a relationship? Not just casual."

Easy question. There had only been a handful of guys she deemed relationship material. Each of them heartbreaking and enough to make her not want to play in that sandbox. "Three years. And I've been happy."

"But you just told me you're not sure how you feel. I think whatever you're feeling now is different in some way. It's not the status quo for you. Unless you make a habit of telling men you want them close. In which case, most men would willingly oblige and you'd have a revolving door."

For sure, the man had a sharp tongue. And she now had a taste of what life must be like between him and his sister. "Did you really just say that to me?"

"Yeah. I did. Not that I believe it. My point is whatever this is between us, it's not the norm for you. You told me that. It's not for me, either. Last girlfriend I had drove me insane. That was a year ago and I've been fine on my own. But now?" He shrugged. "I like being around you. Why can't we let things roll? See where it goes?"

"Because then I'd have to trust that you won't break my heart. That the highs won't be too high and the lows too low."

Again he ran his fingers under her chin, this time tipping her head back. "Your theory is if you go through life without heartbreak you won't suffer the lows. What about never having the highs, either? If you ask me, going through life in neutral kinda stinks."

Sure it did. She cocked her head, away from his fingers, and he took the hint, dropping his hand.

"David, my mom had highs and lows all the time. It was horrible. For her and for us. There was no middle ground. No *neutral.* I don't need that stress. I'm okay with my life. I'm not unhappy. I'm not lonely. I take care of myself. Independently." She waved her hand. "Neutral, as you put it, isn't so bad."

"But what if there's something better than neutral?"

"Is that what you think this is?"

He shrugged. "Don't know. But what if it can be? I wouldn't want you constantly keeping me at a distance because you're afraid of getting hurt. Sitting here, I know before I even leave that I want to see you tomorrow. I like that kind of fire. I want to run headfirst into it. You'd have to want to do it with me, though."

She gazed up at him, her eyes locked on his, the intensity ripping her body in two. Why did everything he said make sense when it was the dead last thing she wanted? This was the battle. To stay steady and not be like her mother. Not allow her emotions to dictate her actions.

But, heaven help her, she wanted to kiss this man in the worst way. Taste his lips, draw his breath, feel his skin against hers.

"Come on, Amanda, let loose a little."

"I hate you, David Hennings."

"I know."

Moving quickly, he leaned over the console and kissed her.

She reached up, squeezed the soft leather of his jacket and breathed in his musky and ultra-male scent while he drove his free hand through her hair and went crazy on her lips, nipping and licking. She moaned softly, the sound low in her throat sparking her brain to overload.

So hot. So…so…astonishing.

Slow it down. That was what she needed. She slid her hand back down his shoulder, softened the kiss and dropped short, quick pecks on his lips, most definitely putting the brakes on.

He eased back, dotted kisses along her jaw and grinned. "Well, that was…electrifying. You may have noticed."

"I did notice. Too much so for sitting in your car in the middle of the day."

He shrugged. "I didn't mind so much. Any time you want to try again, I'm ready, willing and very able."

Coming from the family he did, he had clearly never had a problem with confidence. And without a doubt, he excelled at the art of kissing.

"David, I don't know quite what to do with you."

"I can make a few suggestions."

She snorted. "You are *such* a man."

"Thank you."

Finally, she laughed, the angst from a second ago peeling away. She waggled her fingers between them. "You're good at this, aren't you?"

"Uh…"

"Not the kissing."

"Ouch."

"No! You're definitely good at that, too. Trust me."

Feigning effort, he wiped his brow. "Phew."

She grabbed the edge of his unzipped jacket and balled it in her hand. "I was talking about defusing tension. I was embarrassed and you took care of it. Lickety-split, bam."

He pulled her close again and kissed her. Softly this

time, barely a brush of their lips. Too easy. Natural. And something she wanted more of.

Often.

"I need to go," he said. "My contractor is waiting on me. Think about what I said. I plan on sweeping you off your feet."

Chapter Seven

Midmorning the following day, David stood in the middle of his empty living room while Lexi waxed poetic about the subtleties of the dark brown paint sample she'd sloshed onto his wall. It had some fancy name, but really, all he saw was brown.

"Lexi, it's brown."

"It's not brown. This is more than brown. It has flecks of silver in it. This screams sophisticated. It would be perfect with those steel tables I showed you."

"Amanda!" David called. A minute later she poked her head out of the bedroom where she'd set up her temporary studio. She must have had a rough night because she appeared pale, more drawn than yesterday, and it only accentuated the dark rings under her eyes. "What do you think of this brown?"

"I like it."

"Why?"

"It's masculine and neutral at the same time. Purple, orange and yellow would work well with it. Red also."

Huh. What the hell did he know? "Okay. Thanks."

Before Amanda disappeared again, Lexi held up her hand. "What's happening with your building?"

"Not sure yet. My landlord is working on it."

David cocked his head sideways, still studying the

brown. "My sister found us someone in the building department. I'm waiting for a call back from the guy." He waved at the brown sample. "This is fine, I guess."

"If you don't like it, we can try something else. But I think when you see the entire room with it, you'll love it. Plus, your mom suggested it."

"Oh, then by all means, let's go with it."

Because it would be so much easier than dealing with his mother questioning why he didn't like the color she'd picked.

Lexi laughed. "She'll be thrilled. I'm heading over there now. She's redoing your father's study."

"I heard. The old man isn't too happy about it. He likes his study. But he, too, has learned which battles to fight."

"I love smart men," she said.

On her way out, Lexi stuck her head in and said goodbye to Amanda, who looked amazingly good in David's extra bedroom. He wouldn't get too comfortable with that, though. As soon as the mess with her building was situated, she'd be back in her own space.

After Lexi cleared out, he leaned against the doorframe and watched Amanda press some sort of narrow rubber markers into the strips of clay she'd placed on the skull cast. At some point, she'd mounted the skull on a stand and had added eyes—brown—to the sockets and lined them with clay to hold them in place. Already, the skull had begun to take on life, and something pinged in David's chest. All this time they'd been talking about the skull as an object, a project, but now, seeing it in this form, even before Amanda had reconstructed the face, it had become an actual person.

A victim.

Curious about what she was doing, he took one step into the room. "What are those?"

"Tissue-depth markers. They tell me how thick the skin in each area of the face should be. It's based on tables developed by a forensic anthropologist. Once I have all the markers placed, I'll start adding clay until I reach the right thickness. I'm basically rebuilding her face."

"Now, that's cool. Why brown eyes?"

"I guessed. The hair they found was dark. That doesn't always mean dark eyes, but I went with my instincts."

Seemed reasonable. He moved farther into the room, circled behind her and studied her work. "It's fascinating. Watching it take shape."

"It is, isn't it? It's like seeing a five-thousand-piece puzzle come together." She attached another marker. "I spoke to Detective McCall earlier. They released my sketch to the local media and a couple of national news outlets. He's hoping for leads."

"What do you think?"

"I suppose he needs to try, but the 3-D reconstruction will have much more detail when it's complete. We're more likely to get hits on that versus the sketch."

He scooted closer, dipped his head and kissed her on the shoulder. "Are you ready for a break?"

"No."

Come on. Really? Times like this, being a stubborn Hennings came in handy. "We could make out."

Before he could dot kisses along her shoulder, she sidestepped, leaving him standing there, bent over, lips puckered.

"Are we sixteen? Go away. I have work to do. Work you're paying me for, I might add."

Excellent point. "Have we discussed your fee? Wait. Don't answer. It doesn't matter. I'll pay overtime."

She clucked her tongue. "You *are* a devil. Now go.

Take a ride on that motorcycle of yours or something. Just get out."

Tough nut, this one. "You're throwing me out?"

"I am." Her cell phone rang and she leaned over to check the screen. "Oh, my landlord." She set the rubber markers on the table and scooped up the phone. "Hi, Mr. Landry."

David wandered back to the doorway and leaned against the frame while he inspected the crown molding in the hallway.

"Are you kidding?" Amanda said, her voice squeaking.

He swung back to her. Whatever it was, it didn't sound good.

"That's ridiculous." She shook her head and then rubbed her free hand up her forehead. "Okay… Thank you."

She disconnected and set the phone down.

"Bad news?"

"He spoke with the building inspector. They're saying the building has a mold infestation."

"You don't believe it?"

"Not for a second. Have I mentioned I'm highly allergic to mold? I mean, dangerously allergic. I carry medication with me everywhere I go."

Whoa. David was no doctor, but being a civil lawyer, he'd done his share of medical research. "If there was an infestation, you'd have been hospitalized by now."

"After all the time I've spent in that building, by now I'd be dead."

AMANDA SET BOTH of her hands on top of her head and squeezed. So maddening. And exhausting. Between the stress of being thrown out of her home and studio and having to sleep in a hotel—never an easy task anyway—she hadn't managed much sleep the night before.

This news only stretched her already thin patience and left her more exhausted. "I can't even believe this. There is no mold in that building. All this is doing is keeping me from my work."

Holding up one finger, David waggled it. "You know what? Let's go see your friend McCall. You're working on a case he's invested in. If we tell him you're hindered by this problem with the city, maybe he can shake something loose. Get you back home." He clapped his hands together. "Saddle up, sweet cheeks. We're moving out."

Amanda glanced down at her paint-stained T-shirt and ripped jeans. Her working clothes. "Okay. I need to stop at the hotel first, though."

That got her a frustrated grunt. "Why?"

Had the man suddenly gone blind? She couldn't walk into a police station dressed like this. "David, look at me. I need to change. It'll take two minutes."

"Right. Sorry. We'll swing by there on the way. While you're changing, I'll track down McCall. We have to take your car unless you want a ride on my bike."

"Not now. Later, though. It'll be fun after all this mess."

At the hotel, Amanda left David in the lobby to phone Detective McCall and let him know they were coming for a chat. At her room, she slid her key in the door and waited for the little green light to give her access, but… red.

She checked the key, made sure the arrow was pointing the right way and tried again. Red light. *Deep breath.* They'd given her two keys. Maybe she'd used the other one to get into the room last night. She dug into her purse, found the second key, lined it up and slid it home. Red lights blinked back at her.

"This is totally insane." For kicks, she flipped the key over and tried the other way. Nothing. "Ugh!"

Three doors down, a housekeeper, a young girl, maybe early twenties, who could have been a college student, stepped into the hall to retrieve something from her cart and spotted her. "Something wrong, ma'am?"

"My keys won't work. I'm trying to get into my room. Would you be able to open the door?"

"Oh, I'm sorry. We're not allowed. For security reasons. I could call someone, but if there's a problem with the key, you'll have to go down and get another one anyway."

Frustration pooled dead smack at the base of Amanda's skull and she tipped her head to stretch the muscles. At this rate, with all that pressure building, her head might pop right off her shoulders. Boom. Gone. But yelling at the housekeeper wouldn't help. First, it wasn't her style and second, it wasn't this woman's fault the keys didn't work. "No. It's fine. I'll go downstairs. Thank you."

She charged into the lobby, where David leaned against one of the giant marble columns and talked on his phone. He spotted her still in her work clothes and swung his free arm out in a *what the hell?* gesture. At any other time, if her head wasn't about to explode, she'd have laughed. She held up the key as she marched by him. "Key isn't working."

"I gotta go," he said into the phone. He poked at the screen and shoved the phone in his jacket pocket. "It worked last night."

"Yes, it did."

The cheery desk clerk spotted Amanda and smiled. "Good morning. How can I help you?"

The woman's eyes tracked right, over Amanda's shoulder, and zoomed in on something. Amanda turned and—yep—David strode up behind her, clearly the focus of the desk clerk's attention. He had that way about him. The broad-shouldered build, the dark hair, the close-trimmed, sexy beard. The biker jacket. He screamed bad boy.

In a blue-blood way.

Amanda turned back to the desk clerk, Bethenny—according to her name tag—grateful the girl wasn't fanning herself. She set the keys on the desk. "My keys aren't working."

"I'm so sorry. What room?"

"Five forty-six."

Bethenny tapped on her keyboard. "Can I see your ID, please?"

"Of course."

Security check complete, Bethenny went back to the computer monitor. "Oh," she said. "There was a problem with your credit card."

Ha! Perfect. "What problem?"

"It doesn't say. We were notified this morning of the issue."

"Are my clothes still in the room?"

"Yes, ma'am. We just need to get another credit card from you and I can reissue keys. Do you have another card you would like to use?"

David leaned one elbow on the desk. "What happened?"

Amanda slid her debit card out of her wallet, which was still sitting on the counter from when she'd pulled out her ID. "My credit card was declined, which is crazy because I pay it in full every month."

Every month. Without fail because she guarded her credit rating like the Secret Service on the president. Being so diligent about her credit, she didn't even have a second card to use. In her opinion, more than one credit card led to multiple accounts stacked with debt.

David reached into his jacket pocket. “I’ve got one.”

No! She’d sooner sleep on the street than use his credit card. “Don’t you dare.” Even to herself, she sounded sharper than she’d like and she breathed in, set her mind on solving the problem. “I appreciate what you’re trying to do, but I’ll use my debit card.”

She held the card out, but the desk clerk was busy cooing at David, and Amanda rolled her eyes. Could she not get a break today? *Whap!* She slapped the card on the counter, shocking the clerk to attention.

Amanda tapped the card. “This should do it.”

David offered up one of his sexy grins, apparently enjoying the clerk’s attention. Men. Put a young, pretty woman in front of them and their brains melted. Total lava flow. Bethenny swiped the card and waited. And waited.

Oh, come on!

“Um,” she said, “I’m sorry. It’s been declined.”

Before she even had time to argue—or die of humiliation—David slapped his wallet on the desk. “This is stupid. Just take my card.”

“No.” Amanda set her hand over his. “Thank you. But no. Obviously there’s a problem. I’ll call the credit card company and the bank and get it straightened out.”

And forget about this experience. In fact, she’d pack her things and leave this hotel. With the number of hotels in Chicago, she didn’t need to walk through the lobby again and be reminded of this event.

For two days she’d been dealing with eviction from her studio and her home, her entire life really, and now this? The level of fatigue assaulting her body, the sheer force of it, brought her back to the days following her mother's death. And that was a state of being she didn't want to reflect on.

The clerk pretended to be busy with something on the computer and, yes, her not looking at Amanda and making her feel like some down-and-out slug would certainly ease the embarrassment. "I'd like to get my things, please. I'll need someone to unlock the room so I can move."

"Amanda," David said.

She reached across and squeezed his arm to shut him up. What she didn't need right now was a discussion. Or his opinion. "I'll find another hotel when I get this straightened out. I really just want to leave here."

Getting the message—how could he miss it?—he turned to the perky clerk still ogling him. "Let's get her room unlocked so she can pack."

"Of course."

Sure. The Greek god asked and the woman leaped to action. Amanda locked her jaw closed. They had a situation here and the clerk's only interest was flirting with David. What if he were Amanda's husband, for crying out loud?

Having bigger issues to resolve, she planned on keeping silent. Truly did. At least until the clerk shot David another look coupled with a smile. That, after the embarrassing situation that had just occurred, was outrageously unprofessional. Rude. And it snapped Amanda's last surviving nerve.

Now I'm done.

"Excuse me, Bethenny. You have no idea who this man is to me. If I told you he was my husband, would you stop flirting with him?"

"Whoa," David said.

"Oh, just forget it." She swiped her wallet off the

counter and stuffed it into her purse. "Please send someone up to unlock the room."

DAVID WAITED IN the hallway outside Amanda's hotel room while she packed and took the opportunity to change her clothes. He figured that was the safest place because he'd rather amputate his own leg than risk waiting in the lobby with the desk clerk and having Amanda wonder if he was being a slimeball.

Nope. As hot as that chick was, he had no interest. Zippo. Nada. And Amanda needed to know that.

The door came open and she stepped into the hallway wheeling her luggage, minus black slacks and a fitted white sweater that even under her jacket did amazing things to him. He reached for the bag, his hand closing over hers on the handle. "I've got it."

"Thank you," she said, her voice that normal Amanda calm.

Unlike a few minutes ago when her temper had gotten to her and revealed a spicy side. Twisted moron that he was, he liked seeing her riled. Letting loose. Unfortunately, it had come from him upsetting her, and *that* he didn't want.

The door shut behind them and they headed to the elevator. "I'm sorry about before."

She kept walking, maybe even picking up speed, but she said, "Ugh. Seriously humiliating. I popped off. I was frustrated and couldn't seem to get her attention."

They stopped at the elevator and David smacked the button while she pressed the heels of her hands into her forehead. He should say something. Definitely. Something that wouldn't make it worse. With his track record, that might be a challenge.

He touched her arm. "You know I had no interest in that woman, right?"

"It's me. It's not your fault you look the way you do. You were standing there. She was the one ignoring a guest. I don't know what women think sometimes. I mean, she couldn't have known if you were a relative or a boyfriend. It was just a bad ending to a bad situation. Let's move on so I can get to the bank. After that, I'll call my credit card company." She jerked her hands out, fingers stiff and spread wide. "I have no access to my money right now. Nothing."

He'd love to tell her the credit card and bank situation were weird coincidences. Would love to. Except, being naive had never been an issue for him. Couple the credit-card fiasco with the mysterious mold infestation, and it seemed to him someone had taken an interest in messing with her. In a bad way.

"David, I'm the only one leasing space in that building. And now my finances are a mess. What are the chances someone is trying to get me out?"

Considering it, he rubbed his hand over the back of his neck. "I don't know. Who would want you out of your home and studio? All of this happened in the last two days. Nothing before that? Harassing calls, weird encounters, anything?"

"No. Well, aside from you showing up at my door."

The words came at him slowly, like tiny pebbles being tossed his way, lightly stinging his skin. *You showing up at my door.* The corners of Amanda's lips tilted down and her eyes narrowed.

Bingo.

They both started babbling, talking over each other about coincidences and the skull and the chances.

Amanda held up her hand.

"Sorry," he said.

"It's all right. We're both thinking the same thing. Could this be about the skull?"

"I sure hope not, but if that's the anomaly, it's a pretty decent guess. Who knows you're working on the reconstruction?"

The elevator dinged and the doors slid open to an empty car. Perfect. They could keep talking.

"Your mother knows," she said. "You, your family and their contacts, the detectives, the lab guy, Lexi and whoever they've told."

"I think we need to get with McCall. Everyone else is someone we trust. But McCall. He could have told any number of people."

If the building situation and her assets being frozen happened because of her working on the sculpture, a project he'd pushed her hard on, they had serious issues beyond her current state of affairs. They'd inadvertently poked a sleeping bear.

He watched the numbers on the elevator flash off as they descended and he tapped the handle of her suitcase. If this was his fault, he'd go insane. Seriously, unreasonably, certifiably nuts. The guilt alone would kill him.

"We'll go to the bank first," he said. "Get that straightened out."

"Then I'll call my credit card company. By then we'll have quite the story for Detective McCall. I'll find another hotel tonight."

"Uh, no."

"Pardon?"

"I don't like all this nonsense around you. Hotels are miserable to sleep in anyway."

She gave him the eye-rolling, idiot-on-board look.

"Have you forgotten I can't go home? Where am I supposed to sleep?"

Lucky for her, the idiot-on-board had a plan. "You'll come to my mother's. She's got a guest room with a sitting area. You won't even have to leave the room if you don't want. But I'd feel better knowing you were there and not alone in some hotel."

"I'm fine being alone."

"I know you are, but until we get you back in your place, you'll work out of my condo and stay at my mother's." The elevator doors slid open. "Ladies first."

She stepped off and came to a stop facing him. "It sounds like you're ordering me around."

Of course he was. He also didn't care. He wanted her under his mother's roof. Period. In case anything else went wrong. And the way things were going, Amanda was on a hot streak.

He reached under her chin and drummed his fingers. "I don't like to think of it as ordering you around. I like to think of it as taking care of a smart, independent woman."

She laughed. "Oh, you're good."

He leaned in and got right next to her ear, more than willing to show her how good he could be. No problem there. But, for now, he'd behave. "Humor me. My mother will feed you well and you'll get a good night's sleep. If my condo had furniture, I'd have you stay there." He waggled his eyebrows. "With me. Since that's not an option, my mom's is the next best thing."

Eyes welling up again, she blinked a couple times. Now he'd made her cry. What the hell did he say that had brought *that* on? Rough day all around. He pulled her close, wrapped his arms around her and ran his hand over the back of her head. "I didn't mean to upset you."

"You didn't. It's… Thank you. I could call my dad, but

they don't have an extra room. Neither does Lexi. She's got a one-bedroom cottage and the last thing I need is her detective boyfriend asking questions. I'd have to try and explain all this and I don't have the energy for it. How do I explain something I don't even understand? And you're right here, giving me a place to work and sleep, and I can't believe it. After all this time of being alone, you came into my life at the exact time I needed someone."

So, okay. *Major points, Davie boy.* But this wasn't about the points—at least not totally. This was doing the right thing for a friend—hopefully more—who needed help.

He kissed the top of her head, letting his lips linger for a second against the softness of her hair. "Just do me a favor and remember this conversation when you're mad at me."

AMANDA MARCHED INTO her bank, head held high, mind centered on not losing that last bit of control she'd locked down. Currently homeless and without a studio, and now, on top of it all, no way to access her money. Someone had some explaining to do.

A few customers waited in line for tellers, but she and David veered left to the five desks occupied by the personal bankers. One of whom would be lucky enough to have a mega-irritated, borderline about-to-turn-psychotic customer plop down in front of him.

The bank's ancient marble columns and floors reminded her of all the reasons she'd fallen in love with her building. The one she'd been thrown out of and—oh, her blood pumped just thinking about it. *Forget that.* One issue at a time.

"Good morning," one of the bankers called from her

desk, where two open chairs sat ready for the next customer.

"I'll wait here," David said.

At this point, her life was an open book to this man, but she appreciated his willingness to offer privacy. She gripped his arm. "Thank you. For all your help."

"Give a holler if you need me." He tugged on her hair. "Send up a flare or something."

She spun back to the banker, a woman in her thirties with glossy red hair and creamy skin. A few freckles dotted her nose, and artist Amanda imagined that if the woman spent any time in the sun, those freckles would multiply. The nameplate on the desk revealed the woman to be Elizabeth Nelson. Personal Banker.

Perfect.

Amanda set her purse on the floor and took one of the vacant seats across from Ms. Nelson. "Good morning. I'm Amanda LeBlanc. I have several accounts here and there seems to be an issue with them."

"I'm sorry about that. What's the problem?"

"My debit card isn't working."

"Well, let's see if we can clear that up."

After proving her identity, Amanda sat quietly while Ms. Nelson tippity-tapped on her keyboard.

Frowning, she leaned forward a few inches and studied her screen. No frowning. *Nuh-uh.* Frowning was decidedly not good. From Amanda's vantage point, all she saw were grid lines and one highlighted field.

"I see the problem," Ms. Nelson said, "but I'll need to check with my manager on something. Excuse me one moment."

Without waiting for Amanda to reply, the banker popped out of her chair and hurried to an office in the far corner of the building. Amanda shifted sideways and made eye contact with David, who abandoned his post against one of the columns and wandered over. "What's up?"

"I don't know. She said she saw the problem and then ran off to talk to her boss."

"Ms. LeBlanc?"

The two of them glanced up.

"Hello," Ms. Nelson said to David.

"Hi." He reached to shake her hand. "David Hennings. I'm a friend of Amanda's."

Ms. Nelson remained standing behind her chair. As in making no attempt to sit. Another not-so-good sign along with the nothingness pasted on her face. Not a smile, not a grimace, nothing to indicate…well…anything.

"Ms. LeBlanc, if you would follow me. The branch manager would like to speak with you."

"Is everything all right?"

She held her hand toward the office. "Right this way."

Okay. None of this felt right and Amanda's pulse kicked up. Pressure exploded behind her right eye and she squeezed her eyes closed for a second. Just one second to center herself. *Just get through it.* Whatever this was, she'd get through it. But, damn, she despised emotional warfare.

She rose from her chair and once again made eye contact with David, who cocked his head in question. She'd love to give him an explanation, but she was just as confused. With her current state of unease, it might not be a bad idea to have a second set of eyes and ears with her. A lawyer to boot.

She paddled her hand. "Come with me. Please."

As he fell in step beside her, his long legs and big shoulders moved with such confidence that her panic, that streaming anxiety from seconds ago, vanished. David would help her. Whatever this was, he'd help her.

"We've got this," he said.

A girl had to love a lawyer. At least when he was on her side.

Once inside the branch manager's office, Ms. Nelson closed the door and left. *Oh, boy.*

"Ms. LeBlanc. I'm Mariette Clarke."

Unlike Ms. Nelson, Mariette Clarke was an older woman, maybe mid-fifties. She wore her navy suit jacket buttoned and her hair in a tight bun that created an instant face-lift. Simply put, she looked like a prison warden.

The two women shook hands and Amanda introduced David as Ms. Clarke motioned them to chairs. "Have a seat."

Far from in the mood for small talk, Amanda got right to it. "Thank you. Forgive me for cutting to the chase here, but what's the problem with my accounts? I have both my business and personal accounts with this bank and I can't access either."

"Yes. I apologize for that. Unfortunately, I'm not able to release any funds to you."

Amanda took a deep breath, then let it out slowly. She would not, not, not lose control. But that about-to-turn-psycho person inside her might be on the brink. "Why?"

"Your accounts have been frozen. We received an order this morning."

An order... What? Amanda shook her head, letting the words sink in.

David reached over and squeezed her hand before she could say anything. "And the order came from?"

"Cook County."

He stood. That fast. Just up and out of his chair.

"Thank you," he said. "Let's go, Amanda."

"What? Wait."

"The bank received a restraining order," he said. "Apparently from the Cook County State's Attorney's Office. They are legally bound by it. They cannot release any funds to you."

Ms. Clarke nodded and Amanda gritted her teeth, barely hanging on to that last bit of control. The last couple of days had been a maze with brick walls in every direction.

Clearly in a rush, David held the office door open and waved her through.

"I'm sorry," she said, moving quickly to keep pace with him. "But I'm not sure I understand. Someone from the State's Attorney's Office froze my accounts?"

"It appears so."

Outside the bank, stinging wind clawed at her face and she hunched against it. Her eyes watered, whether from the wind or the ungluing of her life, she didn't care. Hanging on to her emotions, maintaining that brutal control she always fought for, mixed with the lack of sleep last night, left her wrung out. She wiped at her eyes, inhaling and exhaling a few times to let that good, clean oxygen clear her mind. *I can do this.*

At the corner, they stopped to wait for the red light and she faced David. "Why would they freeze my accounts?"

"I don't know. But my brother is an ASA for Cook County. We'll call him and get answers."

TWO BLOCKS FROM Zac's office, David and Amanda entered a café and grabbed an empty table toward the back. The surrounding tables were all unoccupied and would give them some privacy. Thanks to the aroma of fresh coffee and baked goods, David craved a caffeine-laced sugar buzz.

A handful of customers were busy yapping with their friends or messing with electronic devices and barely noticed them. Zac had made a good choice with this place.

Upon leaving the bank, David had called and given his brother the Amanda's-life highlights and he must have made a call or two, because he suddenly had info for them. And by arranging to meet at the café rather than his office, it was clear he didn't want his coworkers to see him delivering that info.

The bells on the door jangled and Zac entered, suit in perfect order, his blond hair equally neat, and David was reminded of their differences. *I have to be adopted.*

Sharp-dressed Zac was the epitome of blue-blood offspring. His overall fair-haired appearance gave him an air of confidence—superiority, really—which he exploited in every way possible. Whether in a courtroom or socially, Zac knew how to work people and he wasn't ashamed to throw around the Hennings name if it got him somewhere. David? He'd done his best to avoid references to the family name. Whereas David looked like a regular Joe in his jeans and biker boots, his little brother screamed wealth and privilege.

Zac perused the place, but with the lack of crowd, they weren't hard to spot.

"Hey," he said, backhanding David on the shoulder.

David stood and shook his brother's hand. "Thanks for coming. This is Amanda."

Zac hit her with the famous Hennings grin, and David damn near puked. He supposed he shouldn't comment or crack wise because as much as he avoided throwing the family name around, he had no problem whipping out his own version of that smile when necessary. At this point, it was a tool in their arsenal. A tool that rarely failed.

"Thank you for seeing us," Amanda said.

"Sure. If my brother is involved, I'm happy to help."

"Yada, yada," David said. "What do you have?"

Zac took the chair between them and leaned forward on his elbows. "Not much. It's a little sideways."

Everything was these days. David held his hand palm up. "Meaning?"

"I talked to the prosecutor who wrote it up."

"And?"

Zac swung to Amanda. "You need to hire an attorney."

Not what David wanted to hear. Hiring an attorney meant the government's case had teeth. What they needed to know was how sharp those teeth were. And if they were real. Because the spooked looked on Amanda's face and the sudden dismemberment of her life led him to believe someone had targeted her. He didn't know her well. At all. But he liked to think his judgment was sound when it came to people and their character, and nothing about her set off his thief meter. He leaned toward her and held out his hand. "Give me a dollar."

"What?"

"My brother has told you to hire an attorney. For the time being, that's me. Give me a dollar and you've retained me."

"Oh, my God. What's happening?"

Zac jerked his chin. "Give him a dollar."

Amanda dug out her wallet and combed through the bills. "I don't have a dollar."

She slapped a five into his hand.

"That works." He went back to Zac. "What have you got?"

"They think she violated UDAP."

UDAP. What the hell? "How?"

"What's UDAP?" Amanda asked.

Zac took that one. "It's a consumer protection law,

part of the FTC Act. Have you ever been involved in a check-cashing business?"

"No."

"Know anyone who has?"

"Don't answer that yet." David kept his eyes on Zac. "What do they think she did?"

Whatever this was, Zac had at least some details, and as much as he trusted his brother, he still worked for the state's attorney, who'd just seized Amanda's assets.

"From what I saw, they think she's involved with a company that buys debts owed to payday-loan places. They allegedly call consumers and tell them they owe an amount higher than the original loan. Someone thinks you helped bankroll a check-cashing company where he cashed a couple of checks. Then, months later, he gets a call from some company saying he didn't pay back the loan and he'd be going to jail if he didn't make it snappy. It's all bogus. The SA went into an ex parte hearing this morning."

Amanda's head dipped. "Ex what?"

"Parte," David said. "It means they don't have to give you notice. It's usually for temporary orders until a formal hearing happens. In this case, they want to make sure you can't start moving money."

Of the list of offenses David had guessed—mail fraud, kiting checks—a loan scam hadn't even come close to the top. And he knew, as sure as he was sitting there, this was garbage. Had it been just the UDAP violation, he might have been able to stretch his imagination and at least consider the possibility. As a wills and trusts attorney, he saw all kinds of financial shenanigans. All these weird occurrences combined? No way. Someone was methodically dismantling Amanda's life.

"No." She jammed her finger into the table. "Nuh-uh. That's not me. I've never been in one of those loan places, let alone funded one. How can they just tie up my money?"

David patted air. "This is nonsense. But yes, they can do it. Asset forfeiture allows prosecutors to freeze accounts they believe are part of alleged criminal activity." He set his hand on her shoulder and squeezed before going back to Zac. "Whose name is in the court filings?"

"Simeon Davis," Zac said to Amanda. "Do you know him? Maybe he's a past client or someone you interacted with."

"Or," David added, "someone who might have a beef with you?"

For a few seconds, she stared down at the table, gripping the edge, popping her knuckles with the effort. After a minute, she met David's gaze straight on. "I don't think so. The name isn't familiar."

"But you're not sure."

"David, I've interacted with a lot of people over the years. He could be the guy who works where I buy my art supplies. I know he's not a client or someone I do business with on a regular basis."

He sat back and rested his hands on his thighs. Annoying her wouldn't help them. "All right. Don't get mad."

"I'm not mad. I'm being honest."

Zac's phone beeped and he rose from his chair. "Listen, kids, I gotta get back. Obviously, this conversation stays between us."

"No doubt," David said. "You haven't told us anything I couldn't find out on my own anyway. You saved me time, though. Thanks."

Amanda stood and held out her hand. "Thank you, Zac."

He glanced down at her hand, and the side of his mouth twisted. "Hell with that."

And then, little brother, being a total wise guy, leaned in and hugged Amanda, the whole time his eyes on David, challenging the bonds of brotherly affection.

"I know what you're doing," David said.

"I'm sure you do, Dave. I'm sure you do."

After mauling her, Zac gave David their version of the shoulder-slap-chest-bump man hug. David had his issues with Penny, but he and Zac? They were solid. Always had been.

"I'll see you tonight," he said. "I told Mom I'd swing by. She's got some invitation samples for Emma to look at."

"Yeah, well, good luck with that."

"I hear you, brother. Later."

Amanda slid back into her seat and waited for David to do the same. "I like him," she said.

"You should. He's the best."

"So, no sibling rivalry with him? Only Penny."

"He's the mediator." He shrugged. "From the time we were kids, it's been that way. But we're not talking about that now. Now we head to my condo and do research. Let's find Simeon Davis and see why he's accusing you of fraud."

DAVID NABBED A parking space in front of his building and as soon as he'd cut the engine, his cell phone rang. At least someone's phone had activity; Amanda's had remained annoyingly silent. Nothing from her landlord on her building or her call in to Detective McCall. And now, with this Simeon Davis development, she'd tried again but was told the detective was on a homicide call. Who knew when he'd get back to her?

"Is it McCall?"

He shook his head. "No. My contractor. Finally. Been chasing him about my office for two days." He hit the button before the call went to voice mail. "Hang on," he said into the phone.

He slid her car key from the ignition then dug into his pocket and handed her his key ring. A simple, worn leather braid with—one, two, three—four keys on it. Her best guess? One for his office, one for his parents' home, one for the condo and one for his car. No clutter of unnecessary keys for this man. He was nothing if not efficient.

"The signal in the building sucks," he said. "Go on in while I take this. Be there in two minutes."

Gladly. The few minutes alone would allow her to make a cup of tea and wrap her head around the current state of her life.

She strode up the walkway to David's private entrance. The units on the upper floors had interior entrances via a doorway that led to a stairwell, but the two units on the ground floor had direct access from the front and rear. Another perk of the building.

With no idea which key fit the door, she tried the first one—no good—then the next one, and hit on the door key. Soon, she imagined, he'd move his condo key to the end, as that would be the one used most often. But that could be the way her brain worked. She and David, though, were like-minded in some ways. This might be one of them.

She unlocked the door, pushed it open and stepped inside. The living room light fixtures had yet to be installed and the afternoon sun offered minimal help in illuminating the room. For now, she'd put the stove light on and hope it threw some secondary light over the breakfast bar into the conjoined dining and living areas.

They'd also have to put a shade or curtain on the glass door at the end of the hallway or people would be peeping in. Frankly, the door was a break-in waiting to happen. All someone needed to do was cut—or punch—a hole in the glass, reach in and flip the lock.

And, holy smokes…

The lock. More specifically the knob on the lock. Before they left, David had checked it. She'd watched him lock it, leaving the oblong knob in a vertical position. Vertical equaled locked.

So why was the knob horizontal?

Lexi. She had a key. Maybe she'd come back after they'd left and forgotten to lock it again. From where Amanda stood, the door appeared unharmed, so it must have been Lexi. Or maybe someone else David had given a key to. That had to be it. Amanda breathed out. Stress had morphed into crazy-making hypervigilance. This was what happened when she left her safe zone. Emotional upheaval obviously made her paranoid. Unsteady.

Need my plain, boring life back.

For now, she'd relock the door and mention it to David. Anyone with a key needed to make sure they locked up before leaving. Three steps in, something clinked—*guest bedroom*—and Amanda halted.

Paranoia?

Clink.

And then a scrape. Like someone dragging something. And that was definitely not paranoia. Unless paranoia clinked *and* scraped.

Whatever or whoever was in there must have been moving the table or sculpture stand she'd set up.

Could be a worker. She didn't know who he had in and out of here. But he'd also told her they wouldn't be working in that bedroom while she was in there. He had, in fact, told everyone to stay out.

A slow tingling crawled up her arms. *Get out.* As silly and cowardly as she'd feel, she'd go outside and get David and the two of them would come back in. Cowardice aside, a smart woman didn't confront an unknown person. She lifted her foot, ready to turn back, when a man, a big man with linebacker shoulders, exited the room. Veins exploding, her entire system came to a state of alert. Her focus narrowed, zoomed right in on the profile of a man wearing a blue hoodie. In his hand he held…*no*…the skull. As if he sensed her, his head came around—beard. Not full. More stubbly. The man's eyes widened. He hadn't expected anyone else to be there.

That made two of them.

The tingling on her arms changed to a full stab, and the chemical odor in the room intensified, burning her nose and throat.

Skull.

She stepped forward and the man put his arm out. "I don't want to hurt you."

"Take whatever you want. Not the skull. Please."

She took another step, but he backed away. "Don't," he said, stretching the one-syllable word to two.

Nervous. She should run. Just let him escape. The sheer size of him terrified her. But that skull—the PD had left it in her care. It was their property, but they'd entrusted her with it. She'd promised… "Just…please… leave it."

She moved closer and held out her arms and then something in her head snapped, something feral and desperate and protective and she lunged—big mistake. The man reared back, swinging sideways, pulling the skull from her reach, but her fingers grazed his meaty hand.

"No," she said, struggling to grab hold.

The man yanked free, spun back and, with his free arm, launched her. Shoved her with enough force that she flew backward as if she weighed nothing. *Crack.* She hit the floor, hard, her tailbone taking the direct hit.

Pain roared into her back and down her legs and she closed her eyes for a split second. One tiny second to recover because—*God*—that hurt. *Where is he? Where is he?*

She opened her eyes, ready to fight off another attack, but the man had gone the other way. Back door.

"No!"

Amanda scrambled to her feet just as David came in the front. "Get him!"

He ran toward her. "What happened? Are you hurt?"

"He stole the skull. Back door. He went left. Blue hoodie!"

Being closer to the front, David tore out that door and Amanda followed him, limping a little, as he charged around the side of the building.

"Stay inside!" he hollered. "Lock yourself in!"

Chapter Eight

David flew around the corner of the building, eyes scanning left and right. There. Blue sweatshirt. A big guy lumbering down the sidewalk. Out of shape. David picked up speed. Easily, he'd catch him.

Parked cars lined the street, and the man ran by them, heading to the corner, where, dammit, an ancient Chevy with a missing rear hubcap sat parked, puffs of smoke coming from the tailpipe.

David kicked his sprint up in case he could tackle the guy before he got to that car.

A biker shot out of an alley and the big guy swerved. Too late. He crashed into the rider and—yow—the rider went one way and the bike the other, both landing directly in David's path. He veered left, intending to leap right over the bike and maybe, maybe, catch the runner. As long as the rider stayed out of his way.

The biker hopped to his feet.

Of course he did.

David leaped and—*oh, man*—sucked a huge breath and readied his body for impact, twisting slightly to avoid a direct hit to the chest. Bam. Their shoulders collided.

"Oof!" the biker said. "Dammit! Watch where the hell you're going."

A sharp pain ripped into David's chest and neck and

he plummeted, hitting the sidewalk flat on his back. His head bounced off the ground, the edge of the grass easing the impact and probably saving him a concussion. Still, his vision blurred and he squeezed his eyes shut, then opened them quickly and refocused.

"What the hell?" the rider said "He could have killed me!"

That might be extreme, but the guy could have seriously gotten his bell rung. Shaking off the impact, David rolled to his side and spotted the idling car pulling into traffic. Missed him. The stream of swearwords from his mouth would have lit up his mother for sure.

"Who was that guy?" the rider asked.

"No idea. He broke into my condo. Are you all right?"

The man stretched his right leg. "Tweaked my knee. I think it's okay."

David rolled to his feet, brushed the dirt off his jacket and took inventory of his clothing. The knee of his jeans was blown out and his jacket sleeve was scuffed, but everything else was intact. The goose egg on the back of his head would hurt later, though. He grabbed the bike and held it upright while the rider got to his feet.

"You sure you're okay? Don't need an ambulance?"

"Nah. I'm good. Wouldn't be the first time I got tossed off this thing. I live around the corner. I'll walk it the rest of the way."

David glanced behind him, making sure Amanda hadn't followed.

And hello…

On the ground right behind him, where the suspect had leaped out of the way to avoid the biker, sat a set of keys. David pointed. "Those yours?"

"Nah, man." He gestured to a small pouch attached to the bike's seat. "Mine are in my pouch. I think they fell out of the guy's pocket. I heard something clink but figured it was something on the bike."

"You got any tissues in there or anything?"

"Yeah." The rider dragged a napkin, one of those cheap ones fast-food places offered, out of the pouch and handed it over.

Using the napkin, David clasped the edge of the plastic key ring and wrapped the keys in the napkin. When he got back to the condo, he'd find a baggie or something to put them in and then decide what to do with them. For sure, they'd check them for prints. It was just a matter of who would do the checking—Hennings & Solomon's private lab or the PD's lab.

He cut through the alley on his way back to the condo. With the darkening sky, he hoped he wouldn't scare the life out of Amanda by banging on the back door. Assuming she'd locked herself in.

She'd better have locked herself in.

He jogged up to the door where the overhead light lit the immediate area, including just inside the door. But his view didn't stop there. He could see clear into the shadowed hallway thanks to the stove light. He needed to get something to cover this window. Something he should have thought about way before now, but the place had been empty. Who'd rob an empty condo?

Someone looking for a skull maybe.

And yep. Back door locked. Good girl. He knocked lightly. "It's me," he said, his voice loud but not yelling.

Would she even hear him? Her head poked out of the room where she'd set up her makeshift studio and he waved. She rushed to the door, unlocked it and didn't give him three seconds to get inside before launching herself at him. A hug from her he'd take any day and he wrapped her up and held tight while patting her lower back.

"Honey, let me get inside so we can lock up again."

She backed up a few steps, apparently too terrified to let go, and that made him want to tear something apart.

Reality was, he'd convinced her to do this reconstruction and right after that her life went to hell. And now someone had stolen the damned skull.

"He bolted," David said. "Got into a car and took off."

She backed away and gave him a once-over. "Your pants are ripped. And your jacket! What happened?"

"He took out a guy on a bike. The rider wasn't too happy when I plowed into him."

"Are you hurt?"

She ran her hands over his arms, squeezing as she went, checking for injuries. The fussing was nice, but if he had a broken bone he'd feel it. He pointed at the back of his head. "Got a bump. No big deal."

"Let me see you." She walked around him, her hand traveling across his shoulders and gently moving into his hair so she could feel the lump. Suddenly he wasn't thinking about hoodie-wearing bad guys.

"I'm fine. You looked like you were getting up when I came in. Did he hit you?"

"No." She waved toward the end of the hallway. "He pushed me over. He said he didn't want to hurt me. And he sounded nervous. I think he just wanted to get me out of the way, but I panicked."

David stepped closer, wrapped his arms around her and cradled the back of her head. "I'm sorry this is happening. Did he take anything else?"

"No. Just the skull."

"Which means he found what he was looking for. And if nothing else, we know, without question, someone doesn't want you finishing that reconstruction."

As much as Amanda wanted to disagree with David's assessment, reality had made it clear that her willingness to do the reconstruction had caused her life to implode.

"I know. There's no way the timing on these mishaps is a coincidence. I'll try McCall again."

She strode to the end of the hallway, where her purse still sat on the floor after her fall. "I checked the locks. They're all intact."

"He must have picked it. Doesn't surprise me with how cheap that lock is. And it serves me right for putting off installing the new ones. Wait."

He patted his jacket pocket, then pulled out a folded napkin. "What's that?"

"This, my love, is a set of keys I think your assailant dropped." He started for the back door. "Wouldn't it be interesting if one of these keys fit my door?"

Without waiting for a response and keeping the napkin wrapped around the end of the key, he shoved one into the lock and jiggled it. Nothing. He moved on while Amanda wrapped her hand around the two middle fingers of her other hand and squeezed. The pressure from her ring sent a piercing stick straight to the base of her finger and she loosened her hold. Damned nerves. Totally fried.

After trying all the keys, David turned back to her. "They don't fit."

"Well, good. Because that would have been another flipping mystery to solve. We need to tell McCall. I'll get a hold of him."

David blew out a breath and propped his hands on his hips. "Hang on."

Hang on? For what? "Why?"

"Let's think about this. Your building was condemned and then your accounts were frozen."

"And?"

"Think about it. The city's building department issued the vacate order on your building." David held his finger up. "And your accounts were frozen after the bank was issued an order from the Cook County State's Attorney. Where's the connection?"

Following his logic, Amanda thought about the administrative offices within city government. "Holy cow. The city. Could someone at the PD be behind this?"

"It could be. I mean, they would definitely have connections with the SA's office. The building department? Eh. Possibly."

"But…"

"What?"

She held her hand up, then let it drop. "I don't know. I'm just…confused. Why would McCall ask for my help if he was behind all this?"

"It might not be him. Maybe it's someone he works with."

"How do we figure that out?"

David grinned. "Hennings & Solomon has investigators. Good ones. They know everyone in Chicago. Plus, Penny's boyfriend is FBI. Between them, we're aces."

"Wow."

"Yep. And based on the conversation we just had, I think we should turn the keys over to McCall but, as a backup, *borrow* one of them and send it to the lab my dad's firm uses. They'll check them for prints. So will the police. Hopefully, we'll get a similar result."

"Oh, David. McCall won't be happy if we do that."

"I know. Wouldn't be the first time someone was mad at me. I'm good with it. But this involves you also. We're a team. If you're not comfortable, we'll give McCall everything."

Not in her lifetime would she be comfortable with

this. Any of it. For three days she'd been in hell. And now David wanted her to knowingly annoy a homicide detective she was supposedly helping solve a murder.

Before her life had fallen apart, she'd have gladly turned the keys over to McCall. Now? With all this craziness, the only one she trusted was David. And he had a plan that sounded, in an off way, reasonable.

She met his gaze, and those alluring eyes of his sucked her in. The man had no fear. None. Maybe she could learn a thing or two from him. Considering that she'd spent the past ten years trying to live her life in neutral. She shook her head.

"I don't like it," she said. "But do it anyway."

He jerked his head. "Good. I'll take the heat on it. No problem there."

Then he plastered a kiss on her. A good, solid smack, more fun than steamy, but a little bit of tongue was involved and she gripped his jacket, holding him in place for a few seconds before releasing him.

"Nice," he said. "We'll do more of that later."

"Excellent. And thank you."

"For what?"

"Everything. If I had to deal with this alone, I'd have had a nervous breakdown."

IGNORING HIS POUNDING headache, David snagged his cell phone from his back pocket and scrolled to Penny's name on his phone. And God help her if she gave him any attitude. In the mood he was in, it'd be war. He tapped the screen and hit the speaker button. "This should be good."

Amanda stood a few feet from him, her back flat against the stark white wall that basically served as a canvas showing off her supple curves. Her hips and the idea of them under him might drive him insane.

"Who are you calling?" she asked.

"My sister."

"Ah."

Penny picked up. "Hi."

She sounded decently cheery, which would only help his cause. "Hey. I'm about to make your night."

"Really?" she said, her voice laced with that special brand of skeptical sarcasm only Penny could pull off.

"Yep. I'm calling to ask for your help."

He grinned at Amanda, actually enjoying the banter with Penny. For a change, he wasn't wondering the myriad of ways she'd make his blood boil. Particularly when he was trying not to lose his temper around her. Most conversations with his sister were a lesson in self-control, forcing himself not to blow his stack when she made snide comments about him running away from his family and the firm. She always claimed to be joking, but down deep, he wondered. He couldn't blame her entirely. He'd done his share of needling over the years.

But now, finally, they'd each agreed to play nice, and like a plug pulled from a drain, the pressure was off.

"Let me call *The Banner*," Penny cracked. "We could probably get page one for this."

"Good one, Pen."

"Thank you, David."

"You're welcome. But I do need your help on something."

"What's up?"

He spent the next five minutes filling Penny in while his ever-diligent defense attorney sister peppered him with questions. As he spoke, he reached his free arm out for Amanda, who pushed off the wall and let him pull her to his side. Whether from being still pumped up from the intruder or simply adrenaline, his chest pinged.

He'd been on his own for so long he hadn't realized, or much cared, whether he had companionship. Before, having someone around meant being smothered, losing his privacy and downtime. Forgoing solitary day trips on his bike.

Having to fill the silence when he'd rather not.

With Amanda, something had changed. When she wasn't close, he wanted her there.

And didn't mind feeling that way.

"Wow, David," Penny said, "you've been busy."

"Ya think?"

"Call the detective. What's his name… McCall?"

"We tried him earlier. He's working a homicide. Pen, not a lot of people knew Amanda had that skull. And it seems convenient that as soon as she agreed to do the reconstruction, her life came apart."

"You think someone at the PD might be involved."

"Don't know. But I wouldn't mind seeing if we can locate the guy who stole the skull before I bring in the cops. For all we know he's this Simeon Davis accusing her of fraud. That's why I'm thinking we keep one of the keys and test it ourselves."

This was met with silence. Clearly his sister didn't agree. Couldn't blame her. As a lawyer, he knew better. "Say it, Pen."

"Don't yell at me."

"I won't."

"I feel like you should at least call the detective and report the break-in. Besides, we have to tell them the skull cast is gone."

We. Not you. *Aces.*

Beside him, Amanda winced, probably at the idea of the skull being gone. He slid his arm over her shoulder. "They'll have to make her another cast. But it's getting close to five now. The lab guy is probably gone for the day."

Penny laughed. "You are great at talking yourself into things."

"I know. It's a beautiful thing."

"Yes, but a crime has been committed and you know it. Let's not muddy this up. Call McCall, report it and turn over those keys. We can still work it from our end and you'll have covered your butt with the detective."

This was what he'd missed in Boston. His sister could be a hassle, but she wasn't afraid to jump into the fray. "I will. But can we send one of the keys to the firm's lab? Pen, I don't know who we can trust. As soon as Amanda signed on for the reconstruction, someone went project demolition on her life. And that's bugging me." He glanced down at Amanda.

"What?" Amanda said.

"Did you notice if the guy had gloves on?"

She pursed her lips. Thought about it. "No. When I tried to get the skull from him, I felt his skin."

"Okay," Penny said. "I heard that. So the PD will get some prints taken in there, as well."

"Yeah. Can we use the firm's lab for the keys?"

"You said one key, David. Not the whole set."

Got her. *Yes*. He grinned. "One key. Yes."

"This makes me incredibly nervous and you know why. If we go to trial, the chain of custody alone could get those keys thrown out. Then what?"

"I know. But Amanda can identify him. We'd still have enough to make a case. There's also the car. He got into a beat-up Chevy. An Impala, I think. It had to be thirty years old."

His mind went wild. Not many people drove a Chevy from thirty years ago. They could put together a list. All he'd have to do is jump on the internet and search images of Chevy Impalas from the eighties. Maybe narrow it to a specific year. "If I can figure out what year that car was, can one of the firm's investigators hunt it down? Maybe through DMV?"

"Maybe. Run that key over here and I'll have Jenna take it to the lab."

"Thank you."

"You're welcome. But if we get in trouble for this, it's your fault."

At that, he laughed. Couldn't help it. Some things never changed. "Sure. Whatever. My fault. Thanks."

His sister disconnected and David shoved his phone back into his pocket. "Wow."

"What is it?"

"Penny and I just had a conversation. No screaming. No calling each other names. No irritation. I'm..." He breathed in, then rested his head back against the wall. "I don't know. Stunned? Happy? Relieved?"

Amanda gripped his shirt. "It could be all three."

He dropped his arm over her shoulder, drew her back against his side and kissed the top of her head. Whatever he felt at that moment, it was...good. And he hadn't been able to say that about his relationship with his sister in a long time.

HOW LONG DID homicide scenes take to process? That was Amanda's question because Detective McCall was still unavailable.

Something that made David happier than it should

have, but Amanda chalked it up to being another twisted experience in a series of twisted experiences.

Two hours had passed while waiting on the detective, and Amanda sat in the kitchen of the Hennings' mansion marveling at the brute size of it. Stylish cabinets and stainless steel surrounded her. The entire space was spotless but not a museum. Strategically placed fresh flowers and family photos gave the room a bright warmth and she envisioned a gathering place for family parties and laughter and meals. During childhood—even now—she would have spread her drawings out on the stone countertops and settled in for a few hours.

Mrs. Hennings set a mug of steaming chamomile tea in front of her and sat in the adjacent seat, her crystal-blue eyes on her. Looking into those eyes, Amanda understood why people caved when Pamela Hennings made a request. There was an intensity there but at the same time a softening twinkle. Dangerous eyes.

Right about now, David could come back from wherever he'd disappeared to.

Amanda sipped her tea. "I imagine your children didn't get away with much when they were kids."

"You'd be correct."

"I figured. You have a look about you. Sort of an 'I can kill you, but I'll use a feather so it won't hurt as much' vibe."

That made Mrs. Hennings laugh and Amanda smiled, enjoying the company of an older woman. A woman roughly the age her mother would have been.

"My children were a handful. All good kids, but they were born litigators. The color on a carton of milk could start a debate in this house." She sat back and crossed her legs, resting her hands in her lap. "Are you sure you weren't hurt tonight?"

"I'm fine, ma'am. Thank you. I think it scared me more than anything."

"As it should. I'm glad you're here. My guest room is in need of a visitor. And David doesn't count. He still likes to sleep in his old room, which I love about him. And it leaves the guest room for you. Please stay as long as you'd like. I enjoy company."

"Thank you. I'm hoping the building inspector will clear my place in the next day or so."

"Such craziness."

"Ladies," David said, striding in from the doorway leading to the main hall.

Mrs. Hennings checked over her shoulder. "There you are. Where have you been?"

No kidding. He bent low, kissed his mom on the cheek, then ran his hand across the back of Amanda's chair, all seemingly in one smooth motion before taking the seat on the other side of her. "On the phone with Penny. And Jenna. She's running down anyone in the area who owns an eighties-era Chevy Impala. It'll be a start until we hear back from McCall." He turned to Amanda. "You've got to be beat."

Completely. But fearing she'd sound rude if she admitted it, she shook her head. "I'm fine. Your mom makes a great cup of tea." She fiddled with the mug, running her fingertips over the handle, an obviously handcrafted letter *H*.

His mother eyed him. "You should rethink calling the police about the break-in."

"Mom, you'll be happy to know I did call the police. Not my fault the detective is busy." He grinned. "And before you yell at me for being a smart mouth, I have a plan here. I don't trust anyone right now, and since McCall is the detective on this case, I want him to handle the break-in and he's busy. I've already told all the workers to stay out of there. The crime scene will be intact for McCall. And it buys us time to do some investigating on our own. Got it all figured out."

"Apparently so. My darling, I hope you know what you're doing."

That made two of them.

Mrs. Hennings patted her lap and stood. "I'm heading upstairs to drag your father from his office. I'll see you both in the morning."

"Good night, Mom. Thanks for the help."

"Of course." She turned to Amanda. "It's the least I can do. If I'd known getting you involved would create this mess, I'd never have done it. For that, I'm sorry."

"Please don't apologize. I'm doing the reconstruction for my own reasons. She needs to be identified. This other business is ugly, but the goal is still to bring that woman home."

Mrs. Hennings squeezed her shoulder. "You're a special person. I hope you know that."

Did attempting a reconstruction make her special? Maybe. Or maybe she was someone who'd lost a loved one to tragedy and couldn't imagine not knowing where that person was or how she had died. The loss alone devastated a family, ripped worlds apart and tore foundations away. In seconds life changed. Forever.

Now someone wanted to stop her from helping to identify this person and Amanda couldn't have that. A week ago, a few days ago, she'd have resisted the case, instead preferring to stay in her neutral zone—as David called it—but now, with what had gone on in her life, she needed to fight back. To not let her life fall apart on her. To take control again and help bring a dead woman home.

For the first time, staying in neutral, denying the highs

and self-protecting from the lows wouldn't cut it. No matter the cost.

"Thank you, ma'am."

She wrapped her fingers around the mug, letting the warmth seep into her hands and chase away the heaviness of the past few days.

David shoved his chair back. "Come with me. I'll show you the guest room. Bring your tea with you."

He led her to the third floor, where the circular staircase ended at a large landing that opened to a hallway painted a muted gray lined with doors on each side.

At the third entrance on the right, David threw open the door and flipped the lights on. The guest room had to be seven hundred square feet. It looked more like a studio apartment than a bedroom. On one wall sat a fireplace with two chairs and ottomans. A small love seat completed the area, giving it a cozy feel. The walls had been painted a deep beige and the walnut floors were covered with area rugs. Splashes of reds, purples, yellows throughout the room reminded Amanda of Lexi's work and she wondered if her friend had been the designer.

"The bed is a king," David said. He pointed to a closed door on the far side of the room. "And the bathroom is through there."

"Thank you. Where's your room?"

Ouch, that sounded bad. Seriously bad. She pressed her fingers to her lips, hiding a smile. "I didn't mean that the way it sounded."

"Then I'd say that was a shame."

He stepped closer, brought one hand up and rested it on her neck as he stroked her jaw with his thumb. Tiny explosions trailed from her hips into her chest straight to her firing cheeks. Something about this man's hands on her made her jittery and happy and...safe.

"You're beautiful, Amanda. Smart and funny, too. When we're done with this mess, I want to spend time with you. If that's okay."

Definitely okay. And if her comfort level with him was any indication, it would be something she'd enjoy. "I'd like that. It's important to me that I finish this reconstruction. Someone doesn't want her identified. She needs her name back. And I want to help with that."

"Does that scare you?"

"It does. For years I've played it safe, not wanting to risk emotional upheaval. The last couple of days? I mean, talk about emotional. I'm sad about it and worried, but I don't feel hopeless. I don't feel like I'll turn into my mother and fall into despair that has no escape. I think that's because you're helping me through it."

He kissed her. Softly. His lips brushing hers in easy strokes, lingering. She closed her eyes, put thoughts of the bed right behind them out of her mind because it would be so easy to fall into it and take comfort from hunky David Hennings. The little explosions happened again and she rested her hand on his waist.

Regrettably, he eased back, smiling down at her. "I need to go. Otherwise, I won't. I know you're tired and if tomorrow goes like I think it will, it'll be just as active. If you need me, I'm right next door."

And, oh, the torture of that. "I'll keep that in mind."

Chapter Nine

Amanda lay in the king-size bed and stared at the ceiling. A sliver of moonlight squeaked between the curtains on the French doors and gave the darkened room an eerie bluish tint. Still, creepy tint and all, any anxiety she'd had about what she'd been through these past days drifted off the second David had driven through the front gates into the safety of his parents' estate.

These people were loaded—L-O-A-D-E-D—and this kind of wealth, the privilege of a lifestyle with no financial worries, was beyond anything Amanda had ever known. Her life, even as a child, had been spent watching pennies, managing money, securing a future. No extravagant spending. No useless toys. Even now, when she made enough to afford a few luxuries, she bought things she needed or wanted, within reason, but the majority of her disposable income went into investments.

She rolled to her side and stared at the doors and the light refusing to be shut out. When she'd come to bed, she hadn't bothered to look outside and she now wondered about the view from three stories up. Fifteen miles outside the city, the property spanned at least a few acres between neighboring homes, leaving Amanda thrilled that this much open space could be found so close to downtown. Of course she'd known, had even driven around the area looking for inspiration, but now that she'd experienced it during a time when she desperately needed to de-stress, the quiet meant so much more.

Giving up on sleep, she tossed the covers back and strode to the balcony doors wearing only her long-sleeved nightshirt and fluffy socks she liked to sleep in. She checked the doors for security sensors. Not seeing any, she flipped the lock, squeezed her eyes closed—please don't let there be an alarm on—and slowly pulled the door. It slid open easily, no sticking like the ones in her building, but that wasn't a surprise. She imagined Mrs. Hennings inspected every detail on a continual basis.

A light wind blew, sending a chill over her cheeks and bare legs, but she stood staring out at one tiny light shining in the distance between a clump of trees. She inhaled, enjoying the lack of frenetic energy. In her building, city life offered traffic noises, sirens and planes overhead. She loved it but found this new and inviting. A mini-vacation.

"Amanda?"

At the sound of David's voice, her body stiffened, each muscle locking. He sat on the balcony in what looked like an iron chair, that eerie moonlight throwing enough light for her to spy him in a sweatshirt over a pair of plaid lounge pants. His rumpled hair, that gorgeous ebony hair, poked in all directions and curled lightly around his ears. The man was beautiful in a completely male and rugged way. No soft angles for him. Anywhere.

She stepped out, gently closing the door behind her. "You're awake?"

"Couldn't sleep." He tilted his head up to the sky, where a bazillion stars winked at them. "I like to sit out here."

She moved closer, then leaned against the iron rail

that spanned the full length of the home. "I can't sleep, either. My mind won't stop. It's so peaceful out here."

"It sure is."

"It's also freezing. How long have you been sitting there?"

"Maybe half an hour. I was about to go in." He grinned up at her. "And lucky me, you came outside."

She glanced back at the door behind her. The one that led to a lovely sitting area with a stocked wet bar and a gas fireplace. But asking him to come inside meant inviting him into a bedroom, one that was temporarily hers, and she wasn't naive enough to believe that setting wouldn't spark a fire.

Then again, it *had* been a while since she'd experienced fire.

She gestured to the door. "I'd like to invite you in."

"But?"

"There's energy between us and I don't want to move too fast. I'm…nervous."

He stood, his long body gracefully lifting from the chair, and the girlie parts went wild.

He wandered to her, set his hands on her shoulders and unleashed a crooked smile. "With the way I feel about you, you should be nervous."

And, oh, that was a great line. At least to her. She so adored a man who knew what he wanted. He had to be a Scorpio. Had to be. He possessed a detached cool, but she imagined an inferno under his skin. One she all of a sudden wanted to reveal because he was never quite what she expected.

And wasn't that the thing she feared most? The not knowing? But with him, not knowing didn't torment her. Didn't knock her off her axis.

"How about," he said, "I promise not to hit on you?"

That made her laugh, a good, solid laugh that came right from her belly and felt so good after her crazy couple of days. "How very gracious of you."

"I'm trying here. Let's go inside. I won't even sit on the couch with you. I'll sit in the chair and you can take the couch. Or we'll slide the two chairs in front of the fireplace. I've never done that and it sounds kinda cool."

That it did. She backed out of his grasp toward the door. "I like that idea. Talking would be nice. Getting to know you would be nice."

"Oh, hey, I didn't say anything about talking."

DAVID FOLLOWED AMANDA into his mother's guest room. His *mother's* guest room. He'd just keep reminding himself of that fact because—yeah—his parents' bedroom was just below them and he'd never had sex in their house. Not even as a horny teenager. Never. His mother knew everything. She didn't even need cameras. Her intuition told her all she needed to know. Pure psychic ability.

Amanda closed the door behind him and as he headed toward the sitting area, he glanced at the bed, covers on the right side thrown back. A right-side sleeper. Interesting. He favored the left. How convenient.

"Have a seat," she said. "Or should you be telling me that, since it's your home?"

"Technically, it's not my home. I'm a squatter until the condo is ready."

Before sitting, he went to the fireplace and flipped the switch on the wall. The flames ignited, softly illuminating the room. In a few minutes the heat would be too much and he'd shut it off. Couple that with the heat between him and Amanda, and he might be toast. Charred good.

He glanced at the bed again on his way to the chair he'd promised he'd sit in, and a vision of her spread across it, bare-butt naked, popped into his head. Hey, he was a man and men had impure thoughts. Sue him. Or sue his penis because that bad boy was definitely coming to life.

Grunting, he dropped into the chair and rested his head back. High-backed chairs were underrated. He hated those low ones he couldn't lean his head against. These chairs? Perfect.

"It's a great place to squat. It must have been nice growing up here. I'd have loved all this open space."

"We didn't move here until I was fifteen. We lived downtown before that. The place was barely bigger than a bungalow and Zac and I shared a bedroom. Coming here was a major shock." He laughed and shook his head. "For the first month Penny was terrified. She was used to her small room and us all being within spitting distance. Being in a room three times the size of her old one spooked her."

"Really? You'd think she'd have loved it."

"Nah. She'd sneak into either Zac's room or mine and sleep on the floor. I don't know how he did it, but eventually my dad convinced her she'd be safe in her room. Sometimes I miss our old house."

"Why?"

"I don't know." *Liar.* He knew exactly why. Realized it years ago, but had never, not once, admitted it to anyone. "Life was simpler then. My dad's career took off the year before they built this house. One case and his career exploded. After that, things changed. He had more responsibilities, my mom had functions and everyone seemed to be running all over. I missed the nights where everyone was home. Penny and I had always fought. She was my pain-in-the-butt little sister, but after that one case, it got worse."

"Do you remember the case?"

He'd never forget it. "The Deville case. A supposedly impossible murder case to win. But my father loves the unwinnable ones. I chose civil over criminal law because of the Devilles."

"Why? Was the person guilty?"

"I think so. And my dad got an NG—not guilty."

"Oh, my God."

"Yeah. The kid who was on trial was nineteen. He was accused of murdering his parents. The night of the murder he was pulled over. The cop suspected he was high and asked if he could search the car. The kid was stoned, so he agreed. While searching the trunk, the cop found a bag. Inside the bag was a bloody knife."

"The murder weapon?"

"No doubt. And my dad got it thrown out."

Amanda sucked in a huge breath. He knew how she felt. Horrified, awed and confused. All at the same time. Welcome to the world of Gerald Hennings and family.

"How did he do that?"

"The cop asked to search the car, not the contents of the car. My dad argued that the kid's consent didn't include searching the bag. The bag was content and therefore outside the scope of consent. The trial court agreed. It went to the appeals courts and they also agreed. If I'd been the prosecutor, I'd have taken it to the Supreme Court. Any reasonable person would believe consent included the items inside the vehicle. Anyway, when the knife got suppressed, the state's case fell apart. Whatever was left of their case, my dad carved to pieces. He's brilliant at what he does."

"But a murderer went free."

"Probably. I was too young to get it at the time, but when I was in high school, thinking about law school, I studied my dad's cases. And that one bugged me. I asked him if he thought the kid was guilty and if so, why he took the case."

"What did he say?"

"He said people were entitled to have their rights protected. His job was to do that. His job wasn't to decide guilt or innocence or which rights should be protected and when. He didn't have that luxury. The cop didn't have permission to search the bag. The kid's rights were violated. Period."

"In an odd way, it makes sense."

"Intellectually speaking, yes, it does. But because of that, a murderer is walking around. And he inherited his parents' estate. A very large one."

"Wow."

"Yep. My dad and Penny love the war of defense work. It's an intellectual battle for them. Me? I'm an intellectual, but I can't stomach murderers walking. My father still doesn't understand that about me. And it took a long time for him to accept that I wouldn't be his right hand at the firm." He snorted. "And then Zac decided to be a prosecutor and I thought my father would go insane."

"That left Penny."

"She was all in. Still is. She loves it. Thrives on it, actually."

"Does that bother you?"

"Immensely." He winced. *Damn, Dave, way to sound like a jerk.* "Hang on. No. I spoke too fast. Her thriving at the firm doesn't bother me. Her working for my dad became a pawn in our battle and I hate that. She throws shade because I'm not a criminal attorney. It translates to me disappointing my dad when she didn't."

"That's a little harsh. Have you talked to her about it? Called her out?"

"Not reasonably. Usually we're screaming at each other. All I know is I need it to stop." He glanced around the room, took it in. "I'd like us to go back to being the family we were before this house. Before the Deville case put me on a different path. That's why I came home. I'm sick of being on my own and I want my sister back."

Amanda nodded. "I hope you get that. I'd hate for the two of you to not work this out. Things in life can change quickly. And forever."

"Like with your mom?"

She nodded. "I'll never recover from that. And I'll always have regrets." She sat forward and set her hand on his knee. "Don't have regrets. It's horrible."

He stared down at her hand on his knee, and the air in the room got thick, unbreathable. But he kept his gaze glued to her hand. If he looked up, into her eyes, he'd break that promise of not hitting on her. Because all he wanted right now was to hit on her. To kiss her. To get her into that giant bed behind them and show her all the things he'd like to do to her. On an ongoing basis.

"Amanda?"

"Yes?"

"If you don't move that hand, I'm throwing my promise out." He smiled. "I'll suppress it. Somehow I'll argue that you've violated my constitutional rights."

Wisely, she snatched her hand back, but she laughed at his corny joke while doing it. "You're a good man, David. I don't know what I'd have done without you these last couple of days."

"It's what we Hennings people do." And that meant keeping his word by walking back to his room because Amanda LeBlanc wasn't ready for him. Not yet at least.

He stood and lightly clapped his hands together. "Now I'm leaving."

She nodded, then stood. Coming closer, then going up on her tiptoes, she kissed him. A peck. Barely a peck. But enough to send the message that maybe, just maybe, next time she wouldn't be so nervous about inviting him into her room.

AMANDA WANDERED INTO the kitchen just after 7:00 a.m., her eyes a little puffy—totally his fault, thank you very much—but she looked amazing in a pair of skintight dark-washed jeans and a lightweight sweater that clung to every place he'd dreamed of touching the night before.

She eyed his steaming mug of coffee and he held it out. "Want it?"

"No, thank you. Tea maybe."

He'd like to take a chance on pulling her onto his lap, see how she'd respond, but chances were his mother would show up any second.

But those jeans…

To heck with it. As soon as she got within arm's length, he hooked his finger into her belt loop and guided her to his lap, where, yes, he had a boner. A good healthy one just from thinking about touching her.

That should have been cause for embarrassment, but… nah. It wouldn't kill her to know he wanted her. He'd probably made that fairly clear already.

She ran her hand over the side of his face and down his beard, where the friction did nothing to alleviate his current state. "This is nice."

"Not a bad way to start the day, if you ask me. What's your schedule today?"

"In spite of the chaos, I have a business to run. I need

to head over to my storage facility and pick out a painting for Mrs. Dyce's youth center."

"She called you?"

"She did. Yesterday. I think I have something she'll like. I told her I'd run it by there tomorrow. Wanna come with me to the storage unit? You might be able to tell if she'll like what I pick out."

"Absolutely." He patted the upper part of her rear. "I'll get you that cup of tea."

She hopped off his lap and followed him to the cabinet where his mom stored all the makings for tea. She had all kinds of stuff in there. Stuff he had no clue what to do with. All he knew was none of it resembled tea bags.

"What's wrong with plain old tea bags?"

Amanda laughed. "Nothing. Some people, like me, do it themselves. I'll take care of it."

Even better. "Go to it. Use whatever you need. I gotta run. I'm meeting Penny's investigator."

"Jenna, right? She's the sister of Lexi's boyfriend."

"That's right. She found three people in Cook County who own a blue Chevy Impala from the eighties. We're gonna scope it out. See if we can find the right car."

"You'll recognize it?"

"I think so. The one from yesterday was missing a rear hubcap. You stay here until I get back. Shouldn't be long."

She stopped messing with the tea and faced him. "Uh, no."

"What no?"

"I'm not staying here and doing nothing, David. Not when I have things to do. Either I'll go with you or you drop me at the condo so I can pick up my car. While you're with Jenna, I'll run to the storage unit and pick up the painting."

His brain might not have kicked into high gear yet, but

hadn't they just, as in thirty seconds ago, decided he'd go with her to the storage unit? "I'll help you with the painting. Don't worry about it."

Whatever he'd said fired her up because her beautiful brown eyes nearly severed his cojones.

"Listen," she said. "I get what you're doing here. And I love that you want to take care of me."

"But?"

"No but. Let's say *and*. I love that you want to take care of me *and* you need to know that I thrive on routine. None of which I've had in the last few days. Part of my routine is going to my storage unit when necessary."

He leaned into the counter and folded his arms. "I understand that. Except, as you said, none of this has been routine. Don't you think it would be wise to take precautions? Like maybe not going places alone?"

"Well…yes…but…"

He shrugged. "What?"

"I don't want you ordering me around."

Ordering. Her. Around.

It took everything he had, every ounce, every gram, for crying out loud, not to blow his stack. Was she serious with that? He'd spent days trying to help her, and this was what he got?

Here we go. The old David, Boston David, would have lost it and started yelling. This David, the new, improved one, was damned sure not going to do that. Not in front of her anyway. As soon as he got someplace private, he'd let loose. No harm in that.

For now, he laughed, ran his hands over his face and sighed. And here he thought making nice with Penny would be hard.

"What's funny?"

"Nothing. Believe me. Nothing." He blew out a breath,

folded his arms again, thought better of the body language *that* conveyed and dropped them. *Concentrate.* This conversation would require a balancing act. One slip and he'd fall right off the edge. Destroy the great start to the day. "Amanda, I'm not trying to order you around. Honestly. Maybe I got ahead of myself. I saw the text from Jenna and figured we could jump on finding this car. Then when McCall gets back to you, if we have something to pass along, maybe we can have him run it down. That's all I'm saying."

He wanted to add that if she felt going to her storage unit was more important, by all means, they should absolutely do that. And then he'd find the sharpest knife in this kitchen and plunge it into his own heart.

With his rotten luck, he'd survive.

"I know you think it's dumb. I can see that. But I've spent my life figuring out how to stay emotionally healthy. Part of that is taking care of myself, not depending on anyone or anything to make me happy. It's been years of learning how to not turn into my mother. Part of that is sticking to a routine. You can't come in and decide you're taking over. That's all *I'm* saying."

She turned back to the container with the tea, shoveled some into a glass pot, then slapped the spoon down. He wouldn't call it a slam, but it wasn't gentle, either.

And, holy hell, that snit was hot. Sick, he knew, but calm, cool Amanda had a temper buried inside her. Good to see.

He held up his hands. He didn't completely understand what they were fighting about—nothing new in his life—because all he was doing was trying to keep her safe, but at least she was honest.

"I apologize," he said. "I didn't mean to take over. I jumped on an opportunity to get something done. I do that. So, how about we hunt down this car with Jenna and then go to your storage unit? We'll do it together."

When she didn't respond, he moved closer, set his hands on her shoulders and kissed the back of her head. "I'm sorry."

Under his hands, the tension in her shoulders eased.

She dropped her head an inch. "Thank you. I'm not easy, David. I'll probably make you crazy before this is over. But I know what I need."

"Well," he said, "I guess we're perfect for each other because I'm not easy, either. We'll figure it out." He snorted. "Just have patience."

She tipped back a bit, rested her head against his chest and pulled his arms around the front of her. "I will. You, too. After I make my tea, we'll go find that car."

"THAT'S IT," DAVID SAID.

He pumped a fist and Amanda breathed in. For close to two hours they'd been cruising the city checking addresses where they might find a 1985 Chevy Impala with a missing hubcap. On the third try, they'd apparently found it, and Amanda's excitement over their success mixed with a creepy feeling of dread. What were they doing? After the break-in last night, they shouldn't be here. Detective McCall should be here.

David angled back to Jenna, who peered out the rear driver's side window. "That's the car."

The car sat wedged between two others in a line that spanned the short block. A car cruised by, constituting the only traffic. Narrow alleys separated the homes, and Amanda focused on the brick-faced bungalow in Jenna's path. A collapsing chain-link fence guarded the home. In this neighborhood bullets probably flew by that fence on a regular basis. The boarded-up home to its right might have been evidence of that. Just being here made the muscles in her neck bunch. Local gang shootings were a weekly—if not more often—occurrence and despite the quiet street, the energy pulsed and throbbed with an unspoken threat of an eruption.

Amanda scooted forward to see around David, and the morning sunshine coming through the windshield warmed the side of her face. "Are you sure?"

"Unless there are multiple 1985 blue Impalas with a missing left hubcap, yeah, I'm sure."

"Okay." Jenna pushed open her door. "Wait here. And turn so they can't see you."

Amanda spun around. This supermodel of a woman with her long, glossy hair, bombshell body and perfect face was getting out of this car alone? Was she insane? "Where are you going?"

This is bad. Bad, bad, bad.

"I'll knock on the door and see who answers. You two pay attention. You never know who'll open the door. It might be someone you recognize."

"It's too dangerous," Amanda said.

Halfway out of the car, Jenna glanced back. "This is nothing. Really. I've been in crack houses on my own. I'll be fine. Besides, neither of you can come with me. If it's the guy from last night, he'll never open the door. The only way to know is to get him to open up so we can see his face." She flashed a full-on smile. "I'm good at that."

"If you need something," David said, "hold your hand up and I'm right there. Got it? No screwing around, Jenna. Just give me the signal."

"Will do. Relax. It's all good."

With that, she slammed the door and made her way across the street in her skintight skirt and high-heeled boots. She might as well be the Queen of England living in the projects the way she stuck out.

"David, this is a rough neighborhood."

"Sure is." He reached across, set his hand on her thigh and squeezed. "She'll be fine. Two minutes and we're out of here."

They watched as Jenna knocked on the door. A minute later an older man, maybe about seventy, with gray hair and a long beard answered.

"Well, that's not the guy I saw in the house," she said. "Did you see the driver?"

"No."

Jenna spent a couple of minutes chatting with the man, smiling at him and nodding. No help signal came and Amanda sat back to watch her work. A minute later, a still-smiling Jenna typed something into her phone before waving goodbye to the older man.

Good. No chaos.

She hopped back into the car and buckled her seat belt. "Supersweet man."

David glanced in the rearview mirror. "What happened?"

"I told him I wanted to buy the Impala. That my boyfriend was a classic-car freak and would love to restore it."

After shifting the car into gear, David pulled away from the curb. "What'd he say?"

"The car is registered to him, but his grandson drives it most of the time and he doesn't want to sell it without checking with him."

Amanda turned back to her. "The grandson wasn't home?"

"Correct. The truly excellent news, though, is, being the kind woman I am, I offered to call his grandson and—" she waved her cell phone "—voilà, he gave me his number."

David stopped at a traffic light and smiled. "No wonder my sister loves you."

"Eh, what can I say?"

How about that she was completely awesome? If they could find the grandson, maybe the police could question him. "Can we track his cell phone?"

"Yes," David said. "Need a warrant, though. That's McCall's territory."

Which meant finally admitting to the detective that the skull had been stolen. The man would be furious with them, and rightfully so. They'd have to face it eventually, though. Might as well get it over with. She dug her phone from her purse. "I'll try him again."

The light turned green and David made a right, heading toward Lake Shore Drive, where Amanda would open her window and stick her face into the moist lake air that would wash away the cold dread that had swallowed her.

Not even lunchtime and she was completely drained. And she still had to face Detective McCall, which she sensed would not be an easy conversation.

Forgetting about the phone for a second, she rested her head back and stared at the car in front of them, letting her thoughts narrow to only the curve of the bumper and how it joined with the back quarter panel. Just a few seconds of distraction to get her thoughts in order. To shut out the stress of the past few days and catch her breath. That was all she needed.

"Everything all right?" David asked.

She picked up the phone again and scrolled her contacts. "Fine. Just thinking."

And summoning the nerve to make this phone call.

“Okay.” He gestured to the phone. “McCall won’t be happy we didn’t report the break-in last night. Be prepared.”

Chapter Ten

Standing in David's yet-to-be-finished kitchen, his beefy arms crossed, McCall had a look about him. One that bloated his face and made his eyes so hard he could snap concrete with them.

David had expected this. Detectives like McCall seemed to crave control. Probably because much of what their jobs entailed was so far *out* of their control. Understandable. In fact, if the roles were reversed, David would have been storming this condo and railing on them, well, as much as he could without compromising a crime scene.

"Let me get this straight," McCall said, his voice low and on the edge of containment. "You caught a guy in your house, stealing evidence, and you didn't consider that important enough to hunt me down?"

"We called you," Amanda blurted. "Whoever mans the desk told me you were out."

She stood beside David, shoulders back, gaze straight ahead, ready for whatever the detective could hit them with. A valiant attempt, but the excuse was lame and they all knew it.

"My foot! You should have said why you were calling and they'd have gotten to me." He pointed at David. "He's a *lawyer*. He knows better."

Yeah, I do.

Again he pointed at David, this time poking his beefy finger. "I'm not happy with you."

Got that message. Loud and clear. And they absolutely deserved his frustration, but if a do-over came David's way, he'd do things exactly the same way because they'd already gotten a jump on the car and its owner.

Giving McCall a dose of his own body language, David poked a finger back. "If you're done screaming, I'll tell you we left here right after the incident and no one has been back since. Your lab can still process the place."

McCall huffed. "At least you did somethin' right."

Having reached the level of nonsense he was willing to take, David pulled the baggie with the burglar's keys out of his jacket pocket. "These are the guy's keys. They fell out of his pocket when I was chasing him. Maybe we can get prints off them."

McCall snatched them out of David's hands. "Dammit. Did you touch them?"

"No. I used a napkin to pick them up. They've been in the bag since."

And the gates of hell will open up to me because I'm a liar.

"We could have had these processed already."

"Hey," David said. "I get it. You're upset. We screwed up. Move on, Detective, because we've got a skull missing and you whining about what we did or didn't do isn't getting us anywhere."

McCall gritted his teeth and sucked a huge breath through his nose. *Seriously trying the man's patience.*

"I should crack your skull, Hennings."

"Probably. But you won't because I'm bigger, younger and in better shape. Eventually, you'll tire out and I'll pummel you."

"Pfft."

McCall stepped forward, getting right in David's space. As if that would scare him. He stayed rooted in his spot, tilting his head down a bit. His height gave him an inch or two on the older man and he'd use that to whatever advantage he could. Even if it was only a mental advantage, he'd use it.

"Really?" Amanda said. "Are the two of you going to fight it out? *That* would do wonders for your crime scene."

Good one. David fought a grin. Call it more of a smirk. McCall huffed and shook his head before peeling off and ripping his phone from his belt holder.

Dodged one there.

Amanda's phone rang and she glanced at the screen. "My landlord. Maybe this is about my building." She pointed over her shoulder toward the living room. "I'll take this over there. Away from the *crime scene*."

"Good idea. We've already given this guy a heart attack today."

"I heard that," McCall said, shoving his phone back into his belt holder. "Lab guys are on the way. We're gonna have to fingerprint both of you to rule out your prints. You better hope we get a hit on this guy. And I'll talk to the lab about making another cast of the skull. My lieutenant is gonna blow an artery."

"Someone doesn't want her finishing that reconstruction. First her studio is condemned. Then her accounts are frozen. It's psychological torture. They're dismantling her life. And seems to me, everything happening is somehow related to city government."

"Please, Hennings. Stick to civil law, because no one from the city is doing this."

Stick. To. Civil. Law. David locked his jaw and fought the wave of anger that shot in all directions, making his legs and arms itch. No better hot button existed, and McCall had hit it.

Dead-on.

Typically, that insult came from Penny, her go-to jab because she knew he couldn't resist it.

Until now. Now it wasn't about him and his need to escape the family legacy. This mess was about Amanda. As painful, as mind wrecking and body shredding as it was to keep his trap shut, he'd let McCall slide on this one.

David shrugged. "You got a better guess? The timing is too convenient. Who knows she took possession of that skull? Make a list. And check them out. That's all I'm asking."

"Great news," Amanda called from the living room.

They could use some of that. David glanced over the breakfast bar to Amanda still standing by the front windows. "What happened?"

"The building inspector didn't find any mold. They said it must have been a mix-up with the address." She held her hands up, her phone still clutched in one of them. "Tomorrow, I should be able to move back in to my studio."

One piece of good news. Sort of. Because jerk that he was, her moving back to her building meant leaving his mom's, leaving safety, leaving him. *Jerk.*

But he'd buck up here and give her a double fist pump. "*Yes.* One piece of your life restored."

"That's good," McCall said. "I'll look into the fraud case. I know a couple guys that work fraud. I'll see what they know. Meanwhile, I need statements from you about this break-in and that cell number for the driver of the Impala. Let's get on it and figure out what the hell is going on with this case."

Closer to dinnertime than she'd expected, Amanda unlocked her storage unit and David slid the door up. Funny, that. She'd been handling that door on her own for three years and suddenly the man in her life—if that was what he even was—decided he'd be the one to do the lifting.

Sure. Why not? As long as she was safe in the knowledge she could do it, she'd let him play Tarzan.

He backed into the narrow hallway, letting her enter the unit first. Inside the twelve-hundred-square-foot space were one hundred and twenty-seven unframed paintings, all stored vertically with foam-covered boards to separate them and allow for air circulation. She'd learned early on that proper airflow prevented condensation and possible water damage.

"Huh," David said. "It's a mini studio."

"Sort of. It's climate controlled and cheap. I wanted space in my building, but the units are too expensive. This works out. It's a pain to schlep over here every time I need to pick up a painting, but it's twenty-four-hour access with security cameras. What did you think when I said storage facility?"

"I don't know. I was thinking a gallery or something."

A reasonable assumption, but economically impractical at this stage in her career. She made an adequate living, but she ruthlessly controlled her expenses. "That would be a small fortune. For now, this works." She grabbed a pair of white nylon gloves from the bag she'd hung on the wall. "The gloves I have will be too small for you, so no touching anything. If there's something you want to see, let me get it. Some of these aren't fully cured yet. It takes about six months for them to dry."

David saluted, earning himself a swat on the arm. She couldn't help being protective of her work. These pieces would make up her income for the next year or two, and care had to be taken.

"While we're here, I can show you some things for your place." She pointed to a set of paintings to the right. "I think the ones you'll like are in this group."

They might as well multitask while here. She'd pick up the painting for the Dyce Youth Center and let David peruse her stock. And since they hadn't heard anything from Jenna's lab about the prints on the key, they were in standby mode.

"I'll get the one for the youth center out first. We'll box it up and then I'll show you some I think you'll connect with."

"What can I do?"

She pointed to the tall, narrow boxes stacked against the wall just inside the doorway. "Grab me one of those boxes."

After wrapping the painting in glassine to protect it, she added Bubble Wrap—flat side facing the canvas—and taped the seams. David held the box while she slid the painting inside and sealed it, attaching a strip of plastic to the top to act as a handle.

David nodded. "Pretty slick, lady."

"I have it down. How about you take this one to the car so it's out of the way? While you're down there, I'll pull the ones for your place. And please make sure you lock the car."

Someone stealing a two-thousand-dollar painting would be the capper to the past few days.

"Yes, ma'am. Got it."

With him gone, she wandered through the unit, checking the labeled racks for the pieces she wanted to show him. After locating each one, she set them upright in an empty rack and continued her search for the next. By the time David returned, she'd found all five paintings.

"Look at you, all ready for me."

Something about the tone in his voice, the richness, caused a tingling hum inside her. Made her mind wander back to the night before when they'd sat in front of a fire, talking. Only talking. At the time, it seemed the right thing. Now? Her libido suddenly made it known she might be ready for David Hennings in other ways.

Ha. She'd never be ready for him.

She lifted the first painting from the rack and set it on the easel. "This first one has all the bold colors you like. It's more modern than I typically do, but I like the red slashes. If you don't like it, we can move to the next one."

"No. I like it. You guessed right."

"I knew it. Already I'm figuring you out."

"Ooh," he said. "That might not be good." He gestured to the painting. "What will this beauty cost me?"

"Three thousand," she said.

She'd give him credit for trying to mask it, but his eyes went a little wide. Even blue bloods sometimes balked at spending money on something they could only stare at. He'd pay thousands for a leather jacket but not a painting.

"*Hokay*. Don't take offense, because I know this piece is worth every cent, but my mother is killing me. I have never paid three grand for artwork. Hell, I'd be happy with posters in my house."

She snorted. "Posters. That's funny. Are you sure you're a Hennings?"

"Honey, I ask myself that every day." He gestured to the painting. "I'll take it. We'll consider it my first grown-up piece of art. My mother will be thrilled."

She smiled up at him. "Thank you. I love this piece.

I'm so glad you like it. I'll get it boxed up and we'll take it with us."

An alarm screamed in the hallway, the piercing wail bouncing off the cement walls. What on earth?

David's mouth tilted down. "Fire alarm?"

"I don't know. I hope not. Because if it is, the sprinklers might go off."

Sprinklers. No. It took a few seconds to fully register. She tilted her head back and scanned the ceiling because—please let there *not* be one in here. There.

"Oh, no."

Outside the unit, the alarm continued its droning whoo-whoo-whoo loud enough to make her ears throb. An icy panic gripped her shoulders.

Get out.

She spun, frantically grabbing paintings. No longer concerned with his lack of gloves, she shoved them at David. "Take these. We have to move them. There's a sprinkler. If they get wet, they're useless. Help me."

A spray of water rained down from the ceiling, and Amanda lunged for another canvas. *Ohmygod.* Her entire inventory was in this space. They'd never get them all out. Her chest locked, all the air from her lungs seizing.

"No!" She continued dragging paintings from the racks.

"The hallway has sprinklers, too."

"Then run," she said. "Please. Get them out."

Each with two paintings, they ran, water shooting down on them. With the amount of water coming down, there was no way they'd save everything. No way.

They burst through the side door of the building into the streaming sunlight. The manager stood in the parking lot staring up at the building, obviously searching for smoke.

"Fire?" David asked.

"I don't know," the man said. "You gotta stay out, though. The fire department is on the way."

Amanda set one of the paintings against the outside wall. She'd find a better place after she recovered what she could from inside. "Until I smell smoke," she said, "I'm going in."

She ran back, David following behind, the two of them sprinting as she thanked her own wisdom for her first-floor unit.

David scooped up two more paintings. "Can we throw something over them? Plastic or something? We don't have enough time to get them all out."

"Maybe the boxes."

Cardboard. They'd get soaked, as well. For half a second, she considered it. By the time she shoved the paintings inside the boxes, she could just as easily carry the pieces out of the building. She set the boxes on top of the racks.

Spraying water fell from the ceiling, drenching her skin, saturating everything in the unit. She shoved two more paintings at David and hauled another two out. They worked together, each trip seeming to take longer as puddles formed on the tile in the narrow hallway. Once her flat-soled shoes slid across the floor and David, his hands occupied with the paintings, body blocked her so she wouldn't fall over. The rubber on his boots kept him upright and once she was steady again he took off running.

Water continued to pound them—*no use*—and she choked up. *No.* Crying wouldn't help. She breathed in, setting her mind on the task at hand. Forcing herself to focus on her footsteps. On getting out.

Later, she'd worry about the loss. Now they'd save

what they could, which wouldn't be much. Even what they'd taken out was probably a dead loss. All her work.

Gone.

Forget focusing. The final element of her livelihood had been destroyed. Whoever was behind it all knew just how to make her suffer. A sob broke free as they burst through the door.

"Don't think," David said. "We'll figure it out later."

She nodded. *I'm not alone.*

David was here. Helping her. Sirens wailed as the first fire truck roared into the lot and whooshed to a stop. One of the men jumped from the truck and held his arms out to them.

"Sorry," he said. "No one goes in."

"There's no smoke. My paintings are in there. Please."

"Sorry, ma'am. I can't let you in there."

She spun to David, her eyes filling with tears, and he grabbed hold of her and hugged her while she sobbed into his chest. The anger and heartbreak poured out of her. Months and months and months of work, ruined.

"I'm so sorry," he said.

"All my work."

Her breath caught again and she backed away and slammed her hand against her chest because…this was not happening. Not happening. *All my work.* She swung her head back and forth and began pacing the parking lot, trying to take it all in. Her accounts had been frozen and now her inventory had been destroyed. *No money.* What would she live on?

Beside her, David fell into step. "Insurance. You have it, right?"

Insurance. She stopped pacing and glanced up at him and her chest unlocked.

He held his hands out. "I know the loss of the paintings is devastating, but financially, you'd be compensated."

"Ohmygod." She doubled over, breathed out, let loose a fresh batch of tears. *Please, with the crying.* "Yes. They're insured."

Each painting had been inventoried, priced accordingly and reported to her insurance company upon completion. The premiums damn near killed her, but she'd been diligent with her reporting. Playing it safe wasn't always a bad thing.

David eased his head back and stared up at the sky. "That's good. Smart girl."

The alarms went silent and Amanda bolted upright. Firefighters lingered in the lot, none of them rushing to be anywhere.

"No fire," she said.

"Doesn't look like it."

David wandered away, spoke to one of the firefighters and came back to her. "No fire. Someone pulled the alarm."

"At the exact time we were in there."

"Yeah."

"Whoever is doing this is systematically destroying my life."

"Unbelievable. Someone followed us here."

She turned back to the building, where the paintings they'd taken from the building sat propped against the facade. *Trash.* She knew. Too much water had fallen too quickly. Which only sparked a simmering rage inside her. This would not break her. She couldn't let it.

Never.

"Well, guess what?" She gestured to David's car, where he'd stored the painting for Mrs. Dyce. "I'm not leveled yet. I have one painting left. And the ones in my studio that aren't complete. I'll finish those and rebuild my inventory. Whoever is doing this will have to work a lot harder to break me."

Chapter Eleven

Eleven p.m. and Amanda hadn't managed to nod off. If she were in her apartment, she'd wander down to her studio and work until her body finally gave out. One of the perks of living and working in the same location.

Here, in the Hennings' guest room, she didn't have that luxury. Here, she'd be forced to play this twisted game of chicken her body insisted on.

From outside came a noise. Something scraping. Something that sounded like the iron chair she'd found David sitting in the night before.

And, oh boy, the idea of a replay of last night kicked up her pulse. Talking with him was easy. His brutal honesty, although overbearing at times, appealed to her. No pretenses, no games, no deception.

She tossed the covers off and once again in her nightshirt and fluffy socks headed for the door, pausing only to shove a brush through her hair. The man had already seen her in her jammies, but she could at least have tamed hair.

At the door, she hesitated. Getting used to these late-night chats wouldn't do her any good. The past four days had been intense and she'd relied on him too much. Tomorrow, with any luck, she'd go back home. Back to being alone. Back to working out problems on her own.

But that would be tomorrow.

She opened the door and a light wind met her. In typical Chicago fashion for wacky spring weather, the temperature tonight had gone up rather than down. She couldn't call it warm, but the chill definitely didn't pack the punch it had the night before.

Poking her head out, she peered left. David must have heard the door open and shifted in his seat. The same burst of moonlight from the night before illuminated him. Tonight, though, he wore a crew-neck sweatshirt and track pants and even in the darkness she saw him smiling.

"I was thinking about a ride on my bike," he said. "It's a good night for it, but I changed my mind."

"Why? Too cold?"

"No." He turned to her, meeting her gaze in the darkness. "I was hoping I'd see you out here."

Oh, the girlie parts loved it. Those babies sent her into full flutter. She stepped out and gently pulled the door closed. "I can't sleep."

He held his hand out and—yes—that would be nice. To just grab hold, as if it was the most natural thing to do. And why not? In the time they'd spent together, he knew more about her than some people she'd known for years.

At her hesitation, he cocked his head, clearly wondering if she'd reject him. If she'd warn him off as she'd done last night.

Not tonight.

Tonight, after a rotten week, she'd enjoy David's company.

Before he gave up on her, she grasped his hand and let him pull her close and lower her to his lap. "Gee," she said, "if I'd known this would happen, I'd have come out way sooner."

"And that would have made me a lucky man."

He reached sideways, grabbed something—a blanket—

off the chair to his left and spread it over them. "Your legs will freeze."

"Thank you. Aren't you cold sitting out here?"

He grinned. "Not anymore."

"Oh, the charm."

"I do try."

He tucked the blanket around her and she leaned in, resting against his chest as his hand moved up and down her back in a slow, caressing stroke. She tilted her head back and breathed. If she could freeze this moment, the pure relaxation, she'd do it. Just stay here forever, surrounded by darkness and chilly air and David Hennings in all his sexy glory.

This moment was made for the artist in her. Only, for once, she didn't want to paint it or sculpt it or sketch it. She simply wanted to experience it.

And that was new.

"I love sitting with you like this."

"Ditto that. And it feels damned naughty, considering that my folks are just below us."

Oh, stop it. "You had to bring that up?"

He dropped a kiss on her lips and she slid her hand over his chest, where even through the thick material of his sweatshirt, her fingers curved over cut muscle. David Hennings logged hours in the gym. No doubt. Seeing him naked, she was sure, would not be horrible.

"Amanda?"

"Yes?"

"If I wanted to move this into my room, what would you say?"

His mind-reading capabilities continued to amaze. "I'd say yes. I've had a miserable week and this is the first thing that's felt incredibly, undeniably right since this whole thing started."

The idiot grinned. "I do love the way you think."

He was so damned smug and confident and adorable that the explosions inside her happened again. If whatever this was didn't work out, it would hurt. She knew that. The man was a risk. A big one. But somehow he settled her, gave her a sense of calm even when her world was coming apart. Something she'd never experienced.

Ever.

With anyone.

He stood, easily lifting her as he went. "Hang on."

She tucked her legs and arms around him, grinning like an idiot herself because this was just too much fun. "I even get a ride."

"Oh, honey, you'll get a ride. Trust me on that one."

David's tone, the soft, sexy rumble against her ear, made her shiver as he carried her through the doorway, kissing her neck, running those amazing lips up and down, under the neckline of her nightshirt and grazing that sensitive spot on her collarbone. Her body responded. Loudly.

Still holding her, he used one hand to quietly close the door—probably so it didn't wake his parents. God, the man was strong. Considering that she wasn't exactly a lightweight. She grabbed his cheeks, ran her hands over his trimmed beard and suddenly she couldn't get enough.

She kissed him and drew herself closer in a relentless quest to eliminate any space between them. Their tongues collided, their breaths mingling until all of it became one intensely sparking fire that burned furiously. If she'd ever been kissed like this, she didn't remember it.

Still holding her, he backed her against the wall, pressing against her, not gently, either, and—*wow, that's wild*—his hands went crazy, touching her everywhere all at once while she tugged at his shirt because she wanted him. Now. Fast and hot and...*physical.* So not like her. The one who liked to play it safe all the time. But something about this man, his presence, gave her a feeling of protection and control and desire.

Safety.

With him, she'd be safe.

Using his hips to prop her against the wall, he tugged off his shirt and even in the dimly lit room, her eyes feasted on a patch of dark, swirling chest hair and the ripped muscles that spanned his shoulders and arms.

"My God, your body is unbelievable."

"Gym. Lots of it. Push-ups every night don't hurt."

He kissed her again and the bulge in his pants—hello, fella—left no doubt he wanted exactly what she did. He tasted like cinnamon and she yanked him closer until her breasts mashed against his skin and...perfection.

He tore his lips away and pressed them to her ear as he rocked his hips against hers. "Tell me what you want."

And, oh, that voice. The one she'd heard the first time through the phone line and immediately fantasized about it. She wanted so much. Safety, love and mindless, hot sex. All of it a jumble of emotions she didn't understand—this wanting to stay in her safe zone, yet break out of it. She wanted all of it. With him. Right now.

She gripped his shoulders, arched her back and closed her eyes, imagining that first moment... "I want *you*."

Always.

But he swung her around and carried her to the bed, where he tossed her on it, grinning down at her as if he could eat her alive, and none of it scared her. With the look on his face, it should have. David Hennings might undo her. In every way.

He dug a condom out of the bedside table and she bolted up, grabbed the waist of his pants and shoved them down, taking his briefs with them. His erection sprang free. The man was absolute perfection.

All hers.

At least for now.

"Amanda, who knew you were such a hellcat?" he teased.

Certainly not me. She slid her underwear and socks off and rested back on her elbows while she waited for him to deal with the condom. His extremely naked and hard body unleashed something primal—rough—inside her. "You bring it out in me. First time for everything, right?"

He liked that. His sexy, slow-moving smile told her so. And being who he was, she sensed the pride he took in that. The knowing that he'd reduced her to something wild and new.

Still standing, he moved to the edge of the bed, grabbed her behind the knees and yanked her closer.

So ready. *Please.* For once, she didn't want to play it safe. Didn't want boundaries or worries about giving too much. She wanted to take and give it all until there was nothing left. No worry, no hurt, no restraint. All of it.

And then he was inside her and the fast, hard invasion took her breath, making her gasp.

He stopped and she nearly screamed. "Does that hurt?"

"No. Amazing. Don't stop."

Instinctively, her hips moved with his, riding the crazy wave of lust, wanting more and more. At this rate, they'd probably send the mattress clear off the box spring, but—yes—this was what she needed.

He gripped her thighs tighter, his fingers digging in, holding her in place as he drove into her, over and over. He tilted his head back and closed his eyes and the look on his face, a cross between concentration and pleasure, made her ache to touch him. To smooth the lines between his eyebrows. Finally, he opened his eyes and met her gaze and she locked herself around him, waiting for the explosion, the ultimate release.

She rolled her hips and he groaned and the force of it, knowing she could do this to him as much as he did it to her, emboldened her, made her lovemaking a little rougher because she wanted to watch him fall apart. At her hands. This man who prided himself on taking charge. Just once, she wanted him weak.

She squeezed him tighter and his chest hitched. Suddenly, her body was a tight, perfect coil and she watched him watching her, their gazes in a fierce battle, that connection so powerful she wanted to hold on as long as she could, not let go, not let it end.

Can't. She rolled her head side to side, imagining the intensity of total release. Letting go. Allowing herself to be completely raw and bare and vulnerable.

Her mind exploded and she wanted to cry out, but held it because, yikes, his parents were right below them. The sound was a twisted, strangled grunt—how lovely—and David laughed at her attempts to hold back, but his reaction only intensified her orgasm. She closed her eyes but quickly opened them again, wanting to see that moment when he was hers. Completely.

He threw his head back, pumped his hips faster and she reached up and ran her hands along his arms, needing to touch him but unable to reach his body as he arched away. He met her gaze again, the intensity pure and electrifying and something she'd never known. This was passion. Hallelujah.

"Damn, Amanda."

He let out a burst of air and she held on as the orgasm ripped through him, his body buckling. He moved on top of her on the bed, propping himself on his elbows, their bodies still joined.

"Thank you." She kissed him lightly, ran her hands over his face, loving the prickles of his beard against her palms. "That is what I've always hoped it would be."

He nuzzled her neck, got right up to her ear. "That's because I'm crazy about you. And to think, we've got all night."

THE FOLLOWING MORNING, showered and ready to face the day, Amanda wandered into the kitchen and found David finishing a phone call. Jenna sat beside him, her long, dark hair falling over her shoulders. She wore a blazer with a white blouse and looked more like an upscale clothing catalog model rather than a private investigator. In front of her were a bottle of water and a plain manila folder that hopefully held something worthwhile.

David dropped his phone on the table. "Well, that was a bust."

He spotted her and slid his gaze to Jenna, then back to Amanda. "Morning," he said, downplaying the fact that she'd slid out of his bed and tiptoed back to her own room an hour ago.

"Good morning. What was a bust?"

"That was McCall."

Ah.

Jenna cracked open the bottle of water and took a drink. "What happened?"

Backing away from the table, he stood, motioned Amanda to his chair and then leaned against the large island, crossing his arms and settling his gaze on Jenna. He did that when he spoke to people. Focused his intense eyes on them, offering every bit of his attention.

"McCall pinged the grandson's phone yesterday. They picked him up, but he's not talking."

"That's not a surprise."

Amanda shifted in her chair and faced him. "What about the security video from the storage place?"

Upon leaving the storage facility, they'd notified McCall of the false alarm and he'd agreed to look into it by checking the security footage.

"That," David said, "might be promising. He's emailing me the video. They can see who pulled the alarm, but apparently the guy's face is hidden. He's not stupid—that's a definite. If nothing else, we can see if it's the same body type as the guy who broke into the condo. Maybe we can narrow both events to this one guy." He held his hand to Jenna. "What have you got, Jenna?"

She flipped the file open. "I'm still waiting on the lab report for the key. They had to bump us for another murder case. As soon as I hear from them, I'll let you know." She handed Amanda a few sheets of paper, then gave David what appeared to be copies of the same stack. "For now, let's talk about Simeon Davis. This is everything I found. He's clean as a whistle. Barely a parking ticket. Thirty-eight years old. He lives on the north side, makes sixty grand a year selling insurance, has a couple of teenage kids and a wife who works as a cleaning lady."

An insurance salesman. Amanda propped her chin in her hand and thought back over the years and the clients who'd come and gone. Nothing. If she'd worked with him, she didn't remember it.

David cocked his head. "What insurance company?"

"A local agency. TRU Associates. They work with all the big companies."

Both of them turned to Amanda, the question unspoken but delivered. "They don't handle my insurance. And I've never heard of them."

"Okay. There's a photo of him in the stack. Page three. Take a look."

Amanda shuffled through the pages until she found the grainy color photocopy of what looked like a driver's license photo. Simeon Davis was a white man with sandy-blond hair, a mustache and full cheeks that indicated he carried more extra weight than was probably healthy. He also had a prominent mole above his left eyebrow.

As a person who studied details, she would have remembered that mole. She thought back over her clients, vendors she worked with, friends of friends, but…nothing. No recall. The thick mustache could be throwing off her judgment. She held her finger across the mustache, trying to picture him without it.

"Anything?" David asked.

"No. If I've met this man, I don't remember it. And I have a fairly good memory. It's crazy." She flicked the photo. "I don't even know him and suddenly he's accusing me of fraud? I've never even been in a check-cashing place. I'm an artist. Everything I make goes into legitimate investments. I keep some spending money, but otherwise, I save it all."

Humiliation over having to talk about her finances in front of Jenna, a near stranger, burned in her throat. David was bad enough, but she'd gotten beyond that this week. Pretty much her life was an open book to this man and after last night and the rather *inventive* things they'd done, she didn't anticipate that changing. Sexually, the man had tapped into desires she'd never explored and that was…well…exciting.

But risky.

Dangerous.

Her face grew hot and she propped her elbows on the table, resting her forehead against her palms.

A large hand—David's—landed on her shoulder. She glanced up at him and he squatted next to her. "I promise you, we'll figure it out. Jenna will work on it until we do."

"And who's paying for *that*?"

David shot up and spun toward the doorway, where a woman, a younger, mini version of Mrs. Hennings, stood. With the resemblance to David's mother, this had to be Penny. A petite little thing—something Amanda hadn't expected considering David's size—she wore a lightweight camel coat over a winter white suit.

The second she stepped into the kitchen, the atmosphere turned frigid. Tension flew off David like erupting lava.

Penny avoided him and beelined for Amanda. "Hi, I'm Penny. You must be Amanda."

"Yes." Amanda reached to shake hands. "I'm sorry we've tied up your investigator."

She slid her gaze to David, who'd stepped back to his spot at the counter, his arms crossed, jaw locked. This wouldn't be fun.

"It's not your fault." Penny faced David. "We don't mind helping, but we have clients. *Paying* clients. At the end of the month, we need to account for Jenna's time."

Jenna smacked the file closed. "That's my cue. I'll leave you guys to discuss this. Because, honestly, I don't want to be in the middle of it. Just someone call me and tell me what I'm supposed to do."

"Thank you, Jenna," David said.

Jenna left and David glared at his sister. "That entrance was necessary?"

"I didn't make an entrance. I asked a question."

David scoffed. "Right."

"Oh, just stop it. We run a law firm. Now that you're about to open your own practice, you should understand we have certain accounting policies to adhere to. And you commandeering our investigator is a problem."

Commandeering? That might have been extreme. Amanda stayed seated, her gaze darting between the two of them. From what David had said, his relationship with Penny was rocky at best. And at the moment, Penny had a tone that was sure to set her brother off. Whatever his initial reaction was, he'd held it back. Amanda could see it in the way he locked his jaw and shoved his hands into the front pockets of his jeans. Good for him.

"I didn't *commandeer* her."

But Penny wasn't backing down. She threw her shoulders back, and for a small woman she had a ferocity about her. No wonder she was a litigator.

This could turn into a bloodbath. And given how hard David had been trying to avoid fighting with his sister, Amanda didn't want her situation to cause a family war. "Please don't argue."

"In a way," Penny said, "you did. I signed off on Jenna locating the car and working with the lab. Those were isolated things."

David waved his hands at her. "Don't start. You'll only annoy me and we know how that ends up."

"Quit waving your hands at me. I came over here to talk to you about this and now you're giving me attitude. Why doesn't *that* shock me?"

And, yes, Amanda could see why David got upset with Penny. That biting sarcasm could be grating.

David laughed. "And it begins…"

"I didn't sign off on her spending all of yesterday morning with you hunting down some car. I came to calmly address that and I find her here, when she's supposed to be working a case for me, and I hear you telling her to do more." She turned to Amanda. "Please don't misunderstand. We have no problem helping you. Not one bit. My mother started this and we feel responsible. But we need to manage Jenna's time correctly."

Managing their employee's time was a reasonable request, and had the message been delivered differently, David would probably agree. He could be bossy, but he listened when people had concerns. But his sister's tone had probably forced him to check out the minute she got snarky.

The best Amanda could do right now was try to defuse the situation. For no other reason than that David had confided in her about wanting to make things right with Penny. For him, she'd play mediator. "I understand. And I agree with you. We shouldn't take over your employee. I've been preoccupied and didn't think it through."

About to suggest that they come up with a time frame when they would need Jenna, she shifted to David and found his deep blue eyes pinned to her. Not in a good way, either. *Venom.* Her arms tingled and she sat up a little.

"And what?" he said. "It's *my* fault now?"

WASN'T THIS DANDY? Amanda taking Penny's side. Over the most idiotic thing. And what really chapped him was that he shouldn't lose it over this, shouldn't let his hang-ups over always being the odd man out get to him. He'd promised himself he'd work on getting along with Penny, to not let her bait him into arguments, because she knew, as well as he did, she had a knack for firing his temper.

He'd accepted the rules of the game years ago, accepted the mind-messing toll it took, accepted that he and Penny would always compete. Sometimes viciously. Those things he got. But what he didn't get was how, after he'd been idiot enough to confide in Amanda about his relationship with Penny, not to mention his insecurities over being the outsider of his family, she could side with his sister.

Against him.

He'd trusted her. And what did he get out of it? A night of great sex and her discounting everything he'd done for her in the past few days.

Damn, this ripped him.

"Whoa," she said, her eyes catching fire. "I didn't say it was your fault."

"Well, honey, it sure sounded like it."

"Oh, come on, David."

"Come on what? I've been running my tail off trying to help you, and my sister walks in and all of a sudden you two are allies."

Drama Queen Penny threw her hands up and huffed. "Every time. Every damned time I try to have a conversation with you and think we can get along, you throw a hissy fit."

"Are you insane?" Amanda said, talking over Penny and—damn—the wheels were coming off this truck fast. "I'm not taking anyone's side. But, God help me, I can see why you two have issues."

Ignoring Amanda, he went back to Penny. "You're the one who walks around here smarting off at everyone. Why Dad and Zac let you get away with it, I have no idea. You're not twelve anymore. Grow the hell up."

The corner of her mouth lifted, but it wasn't a smile. Far from it. What he had here was more of a resigned sadness with some smug thrown in.

"There's the brother I know. I wondered how long it would take."

"Oh, David," Amanda said. "You don't mean that."

No. He didn't. But, dang it, they'd gotten him riled up, never hard with Penny, and he'd lost his temper.

"Sure he does," Penny said. "Because despite all this garbage he's been feeding me about wanting to improve our relationship, my brother simply doesn't like me. He may love me, but he doesn't like or respect me."

He glanced behind him at the knife rack next to the stove, contemplated the handle on the carving knife, pictured it protruding from his chest. After he'd put it there. That would break his mother's heart. Bad plan. He turned back to his sister. "Now I don't like you? Do me a favor, don't tell me what I don't like."

"Whatever, David. But if you want to use the firm's investigators, you need to ask. That's all I came here to tell you."

Penny marched out and for a few seconds he considered chasing after her. Experience had taught him that wouldn't go well. For either of them. When they fought, it took a couple of hours for reason to grab hold again. So he'd wait. Maybe talk to her later.

"Well," Amanda said, "I see what you meant about you two."

He squeezed his eyes closed and ran the palms of his hands over his head because his rising blood pressure gave him a damned headache. "Yeah. That was classic Penny and David. A couple of dopes. But I needed you on my side."

"I am on your side."

Could have fooled him. "By agreeing with her?"

"I didn't agree with her. All I said—"

"Hold up. I've told you what life is like in this family. I'm the rebel. I don't think it's a lot to ask of you to support me."

She craned her neck forward, then let her head drop

half an inch. Incredulous. That was what she was. Clearly, he was speaking another language, because she didn't get it.

"David, I'm assuming you're keyed up right now because I *cannot* believe you're blaming me for this. All I said was I understood what she was saying."

"Yeah, but you don't know her. She'll use that as ammunition. And I'm sick of that. I'm sick of everything I say turning into a fight. So, if you and I are gonna work, you need to be Team David."

"And you don't think that's ridiculous?"

Hell no. Even if it was, that was reality. "It's how things work around here. In a house full of attorneys, either you win or you lose. I need to be able to count on you. If this is gonna work, you've gotta have my back. Whether I'm wrong or right we can talk about later, but when it comes to my sister, you're on my side."

She sat back, her shoulders slumping, her body nearly folding over, and whatever she intended to say, it wouldn't be good for him.

"Wow. If that's the way you operate, you people are brutal. Seriously, brutal. Whether you believe it or not, I am on your side. But there will be times when I don't agree with you. It doesn't mean I'm not supportive." She slid out of her chair. "That's a lesson both you and your sister need to learn. It's not about sides. It's about figuring out how to work together."

She pushed the chair in, then kept her grip on the top of it for a few seconds, and the raging pain at the base of his neck shot straight into his head. The next few seconds would be bad. He knew it.

She let go of the chair and faced him, her eyes not nearly as fiery as before. What he saw now was worse.

This droopy sadness might kill him. *Where's that carving knife?*

"You can call me when you learn that lesson because I can't have this. I've said all along I don't want the drama. Emotionally, it'll destroy me. And I know what that looks like. I won't risk it. Now I have a painting to deliver."

What the hell was she doing? They'd had a fight. After one argument she wanted to turn tail? Nuh-uh. Not happening. "That's it? End of discussion?"

By the time she got to the hallway, he was on her. "Amanda, hang on."

"No, David. One thing I won't do is *hang on*. You've made it clear what you need. I can choose not to give you what you need."

"I don't want you going alone."

"I don't really care what you want. I'll be back to pick up my things later. So, yes, I believe this *is* the end of it."

AMANDA CLIMBED INTO her car, her body going through the motions of starting the engine, shifting the car into gear, pressing the gas pedal and maneuvering down the winding driveway. If she concentrated on the task, focused on each individual element, she wouldn't come apart.

All along she'd been right. Living in neutral might not have been exciting, but it wasn't this, either. This agonizing stab of heartbreak. But this was what happened when people opened up, trusted others and allowed them in. Fell in love. Which, darn it, sounded stupid after only a few days, but if she could force herself to believe she had fallen in love, she wouldn't feel so crummy right now. She'd have an explanation other than her own stupidity.

She banged the steering wheel—boom, boom, boom.

Ow. That last one sent a shock of pain tearing right up her arm.

Her throat locked up, just a vicious clog of air that wouldn't let loose, and her eyes filled with tears. *Darn it.* She hated crying. But why not? Might as well cry it out.

The road ahead blurred. She swiped at her tears and eased the car to the side of the road, the tires crunching over gravel that lined the shoulder. From the floorboard in the backseat, the box with her painting—her only remaining completed work—shifted and she spun to check it.

It's fine. Everything would be fine. She'd give herself a couple of minutes to cry it out. To wail like an infant because she was alone and no one would know and she wouldn't have to be humiliated.

Maybe, for once, a good cry would do her good.

Except her phone rang. Of course. Lexi. Probably checking on her. She'd been giving Lexi daily updates on the goings-on, and besides David, Lexi was the only other person who knew the whole of it. With Lexi, there'd be no bringing her up to speed. This call she would most definitely answer. "Hi. Where are you?"

"My office. Why?"

"Can I come over? I need a friend."

"My goodness, Amanda, in all the time I've known you, I don't think I've ever heard you say that."

"That's because I never have."

DAVID STOOD IN his mother's kitchen, hands on hips as he stared out the back window. How long should he wait to call Amanda? If she were anything like him and Penny—and wasn't getting involved with a woman like his sister a thought that gave him stomach cramps?—she needed a cooling-off period. Chances were, as ornery as she'd looked when she'd walked out, she probably wouldn't answer his call.

What he should have done was gone after her. Even if she had said she didn't want him to. After the past few days, it wasn't safe for her to be out alone.

He kicked his foot out, just missing the doorframe because his mother would crucify him if he did any damage. There wasn't one damn thing to punch or pummel or pulverize, and all that frustration sizzled inside him like acid on skin.

"Oh, my," his mother said, entering the kitchen. "What now?"

Terrific. Add her to the pile. What else could be thrown at him today?

"Women," he said. "That's what. If I live to be a hundred, I'll never figure your gender out."

Mom laughed. Laughed. Seriously?

"Your *gender*? David, you make us sound like we live to torment you."

Yeah, well. *He* wouldn't be the one to say it.

He turned from the window. "Mom, you have to be straight with me and tell me I'm adopted. It would explain a lot. Because I sure as hell do not have the people skills I need to survive this family."

She cocked her head, narrowed her gaze in that all-knowing-mother way. "You're the spitting image of your father. Chances are, you're not adopted. Furthermore, I think your people skills are fine. But whatever is bothering you, sit down and tell your mother about it. I'll heat you up a brownie. That always helped when you were little."

Brownies. In the morning. Excellent.

From the cabinet next to the fridge, she pulled out a plastic container and a paper plate. "I made them yesterday and hid them. Between you and your father, they wouldn't have lasted an hour."

She popped the brownie into the microwave. "I suppose you want a glass of milk?"

Yep. His mother knew him. "I'll get it," he said.

She shooed him away. "Sit. You've had a long few days. And I don't get to mother the three of you anymore. I miss those days."

"I know you do. Damned kids always have to grow up."

And fight.

He dropped into the chair and rubbed the palms of his hands into his eye sockets. "Mom, I'm tired of arguing."

"My darling, you come from a family filled with litigators. I don't think the arguing will end soon. You have to do what I've done and learn to work around it."

Ha. Good one. "How?"

"Practice. Years of it. Don't get upset with me, but your way of dealing with the issues you have with Penny, and to a certain extent, your father, is to escape. You moved to Boston. And I don't blame you. You're entitled to live your life the way you choose. But I think you've realized you can only hide for so long. Now you're back. And I think you'll be much happier if you stop letting your sister frustrate you. I swear I could knock your heads together. The two of you can barely be in a room together without one of you picking at the other. One of you starts and the other always bites."

"She usually starts."

She rolled her eyes and scoffed. "Very mature. You do your share."

He grunted. But no argument materialized because yeah, he tended to strike, as he'd just done, in anticipation of Penny getting snarky with him. Dammit.

Mom set a giant glass of milk and a warm brownie in front of him. "You know, Zac loves brownies, too. He likes ice cream on his, though, while you like them plain."

"What about Penny?"

"No. She's gummy bears. Buy her a bag and she'll love you forever."

Gummy bears. How did he not know that? Shouldn't he have known that? Sure, he'd been living away for a few years, but still, he could have taken an interest in the things his sister liked. And not taking that interest, in his humble opinion, made him someone he didn't want to be.

He slouched back and shook his head. "I'm a jerk."

Mom set her hand on his shoulder and kissed the top of his head. "We're all jerks sometimes. Take your sister gummy bears and tell her you're done fighting and poking at her."

"I already did that at dinner the other night. Sort of."

"Well, make this one definitive. After that, it'll be up to her to do the same. The two of you can get along. You've just never figured out how to not antagonize. My suggestion? Go to lunch alone with her once a week. You'll probably find the two of you have a lot in common. I know I see it. You just don't know each other, David. And, God help me, it's wearing me out."

He shifted in his chair and stared up at his mother. "I'm sorry, Mom."

"I know you are. But fix it. Please."

"We will."

"And I saw Amanda leave here without you. You're on a roll, my boy. Whatever that was about, you need to fix that, too. I've got my eye on her for the next member of this family."

David cracked up. "Hey!"

Mom held her hands up as she left the room. "That's all I'm saying. Just fix it."

His mother made it sound so easy. As if years of he and Penny ripping at each other could be fixed with one conversation.

If it could, he'd be in great shape because not only would it eliminate the jealousy and competitiveness with Penny, but also it would score him points with Amanda.

And after the fight he'd just had with both of them—*way to multitask, Davey*—he needed both.

The plan on how to make that happen started with conversations with both of them. He slugged the last of the milk and his brownie, slouched back in his chair, stretched his legs and studied his boots while the low hum of the fridge knocked his blood pressure down a few hundred notches. A ride on his bike, a couple hours to check out and breathe, would do him good about now. What a damned start to the day.

But, as his mother had said, he could fix it.

He'd call Penny first. Then Amanda. But he knew his sister, and she hadn't had her two-point-five hours to cool down. If he tried her now, she'd still be in viper mode and that wouldn't play well.

He picked up his phone and tapped at the screen to call Amanda. It came as no surprise that the call went to voice mail. After four rings. Meaning, the lovely Amanda LeBlanc was PO'd at him and ignored his call. He'd let that ride for Penny's requisite two-point-five hours, too. Get them both after a cool-down period. But he'd leave her a message—an apology—and hope to hell she was the forgiving type.

He set his phone aside and flipped open the file Jenna had given him on Simeon Davis. The first page gave the basic who, what and when and David perused it.

He scanned the address—west side of Chicago—and checked the time. Chances were the insurance office where old Simeon worked would open around nine, and with the morning traffic, he could get there right about that time. How convenient. He'd take it as a sign that a small *chat* with Simeon was in order.

He scooped up the file and grabbed his favorite jacket, the Belstaff, which had taken the beating. Completely annoying. Add that to his list of complaints about this whole mess. Just another reason—albeit a minor one—to find out who was behind all this.

Or maybe, as his sister had said, he was good at talking himself into things. Either way, he'd pay Simeon Davis a call.

Chapter Twelve

Amanda walked into Lexi's garage-turned-office, a place she'd designed herself, and plopped onto the sofa in front of the desk. Who put a sofa in front of a desk? Lexi, that was who. Because it was her office and she could do with it as she pleased. She scanned the muted yellow walls and the shiny bookshelves loaded with design books and catalogs and samples and marveled at the change the place had undergone. A few months ago it had been filled with junk from the previous owner, and now it belonged in a home magazine.

"I can't believe this was once a garage. From inside you'd never know it."

Lexi sat back in her desk chair and took in the room. "Thank you. I'm so happy it's finally done. I knew when I bought this place I could make an office out of it. And the best is I can pull my car into the alley and open the bay door to load and unload it. No more schlepping those gigantic sample books if I can't find parking on my block. But you're not here to talk about my garage. You look a mess. What's going on?"

"And here I thought I cleaned myself up before coming in here."

Lexi shrugged. "You probably did, but I've never seen

you cry, so I know just by looking at your blotchy skin you had a good jag."

"It's been a rough week."

"Are you back in your place yet?"

"No. Hopefully today. The landlord got that worked out. The building department said it was a mix-up. I'd believe that if the skull hadn't gotten stolen, my bank accounts weren't frozen and my paintings weren't ruined." She let out a sarcastic grunt. "I'm my own reality television show."

Lexi leaned forward and held her hand out. "Honey, I'm so sorry this is happening to you."

Amanda took her hand, thankful for a friend to talk with. Something she hadn't done nearly enough. The fact that she had few true friends might be the reason, but that was her own fault. She had plenty of acquaintances, but people to share the details of her life with, secrets and fears, she didn't seek out. Doing that required emotional investments and, well…that was that.

Such a waste.

"And I haven't told you the best part," Amanda said.

"You can top all that's happened?"

"David Hennings."

Lexi drew her eyebrows in and Amanda rolled her hand. *Come on, Lex, you know.*

It took a few seconds, but Lexi's mouth dropped open. An all-around amusing look for the always cool and put-together interior designer.

"You and *David*?" She smacked her hand on the desk. "Good for you. The man is hotter than a two-dollar pistol."

Having always suspected Lexi might be insane, she thought this only proved it. How the hell was all this upheaval a good thing? "No. Not good for me. Not good at all. He's so, well, *hot*. In every way, if you know what I mean."

Lexi hooted. "I can't believe it. This is great."

She didn't understand. "It's not great. We're days into this and I'm already sad. Lexi, these people are crazy. I mean, they thrive on drama."

"Well, yeah, but it works for them." Lexi drew up, apparently thinking. "Ooohhhhh," she said. "Now I get it."

"Yes. I can't have that." She waved her hands in front of her chest. "It gets me too churned up. Like I don't know what to do with all these feelings. I've spent a long time building a life and I liked that life. Now the Hennings clan comes along and it all crumbles. And worse, I let myself have feelings for him and I'm already crying."

"Just hold on a second. You just said you'll be back in your place today. With that alone you're putting your life back together. I can promise you the fraud case will go away. It's a crock and you've got the best legal minds in the city on your side." Lexi leaned into her elbows on the desk, her gaze direct but filled with understanding. "I'm not minimizing what you've been through. It's a nightmare. Unfortunately, as you know, this is life. Bad stuff happens to good people. You rely on those who care about you to help you get out of that bad stuff. It's the way things work. You've just never let yourself have that. That's a shame if you ask me. Then again, what do I know?"

Apparently, she knew a lot. "Gee, Lex, don't hold back. Please. Be honest."

Lexi laughed. "I just think it would be nice to see you take a risk. And David is the perfect candidate. He's—"

"Not a conformist."

"Yes! He's a little unpredictable. Not what you'd think

of someone coming from his family. And, well, let's face it, he's nice to look at."

And he's great in bed. "I don't know, Lex. The intensity scares me."

"Of course it does. That's what's supposed to happen. But it should be a good scary. Don't you remember how I was when I met Brodey?"

"Total man hater."

"Ew. It sounds so harsh, but yes, true. He was different, though. I needed him in my life. He proved to me that he could be trusted. Neither of us is perfect and we've definitely been tested, but we got through it."

She glanced around the garage, the very place where a murderer had trapped her just a few months ago. But Brodey had shown up and the two of them, together, had overpowered the man. She brought her gaze back to Amanda. "What I went through in here was horrible. I still don't sleep well. But if there's one good thing that came out of it, it's that I know Brodey will always take care of me. Even when we're mad at each other. And I think you have to go through the tough stuff to really see a person's character."

"Even when he and his family are a little nuts?"

Lexi laughed. "Especially then. Did you forget my boyfriend's sister works for these people? Believe me, Jenna tells Brodey all the stories and we're not talking cray-cray here. They're *excitable*. But Jenna loves them. And yes, she talks about Penny and how loony she is, but she's a good person and incredibly loyal. They all are. Maybe..."

She hesitated and uh-oh. Amanda knew whatever would come next might hurt. "What?"

"I adore you. You know that. So anything I say is because I care. It's not meant—"

"Oh, just say it already."

Lexi laughed. "Fine. I think you're too stringent with the way you live your life. You're always afraid of the next bad thing. It has to be exhausting."

"You have no idea."

Again, Lexi smacked her hand on the desk. "My point exactly. A guy like David might be the perfect balance for you. He's a risk taker and you're not."

"You're saying I should lighten up a little?"

"Honey, you should lighten up *a lot*. Imagine the fun you'd have."

TRU INSURANCE. That was what the imprint on the door of the glass storefront said. Not what David had expected, but he could say that about the entire past four days. Standing on the sidewalk, the clouds overhead breaking up but not yet letting the sun through to warm the air, he glanced in both directions. At least two of the stores within his sight were empty, their windows showcasing a for-lease sign. The lack of foot traffic—there weren't even a lot of cars driving by—didn't bode well, but it was still early on a Friday morning. Maybe things picked up later in the day.

Whoever did their prospecting might need a lesson or two on choosing a great office location. An insurance company didn't necessarily need foot traffic, but it never hurt. Or maybe rent was cheap because of the lack of pedestrian traffic and that was why TRU Insurance chose this location.

Did it matter? Hell if he knew. He might find out in the next ten minutes, though.

He pulled open the door and found a young redhead sitting at the first desk with a plaque that said RECEPTIONIST. There you go. Even if he found it bogus that the woman's name wasn't even on the plaque. Would it be so hard to put *Mary Jones, Receptionist* on there?

Not his problem. He glanced around at the four empty desks behind Mary Jones, the name she would forever be known as. They were standard-issue circa 1970s cheap metal, and combining them with the location, David got the feeling TRU Insurance wasn't exactly a huge money-maker. The hallway behind the desks led to a couple of doors and dead-ended at the rear entrance.

"Good morning," Mary Jones said.

"Hi."

"Can I help you?"

"I'm looking for Simeon Davis."

Mary popped out of her chair. "He's right in the back. Who should I say is calling?"

He could and probably should give a fake name, but—the *but* always got him in trouble—why bother? If Simeon didn't know Amanda, he wouldn't know David, either. If he did know Amanda, maybe he'd have gotten wind that David had been her sidekick all week.

Going with that theory and assuming Simeon was aware of David's connection to Amanda, he figured it wouldn't hurt for him to know they'd tracked him down.

Rather easily.

Plus, the Hennings name was legendary in this town. That alone might scare the pants off the guy.

Finally, he wasn't here to harass. Depending on your definition of harassment. All he wanted was to deliver a message—a very strong one—to Simeon Davis. Who-ever the hell he was.

Decision made.

"I'm David Hennings."

Mary Jones, a pretty young thing for sure, scampered

off and a minute later came back, followed by a man who looked like the photo Jenna had shared. He drew closer and David spotted the telltale mole above his eye.

"Hello." The man smiled—total greasy car salesman—and extended his hand. "I'm Simeon. How can I help you?"

David shook his hand. "David Hennings. Is there somewhere we can talk?"

"Of course. My desk."

Okay. That worked. He trailed him to the last desk on the right. Apparently assuming this was a business meeting, Simeon took a legal pad from the drawer and grabbed a pen from a leather pencil cup on top of the desk.

Pen at the ready, he nodded. "What can I help you with?"

"Amanda LeBlanc."

He cocked his head and pursed his lips. "I don't follow."

Now, this was interesting. By the look on his face, either the guy was a great liar or he didn't know Amanda. At all. Not even by name. "You accused her of fraud and had her assets frozen."

Game over.

Simeon's shoulders shot back against his creaky chair. "I'm sorry. I can't help you."

He made a move to get up and David beat him to it by standing and blocking his path. He kept his hands loose at his sides. Nonthreatening, but readily available. "I didn't expect you to help me. I'm going to help you, though, and give you things to think about. Like how badly you want to be incarcerated. Because whatever this fraud nonsense is, you'll have to prove the allegations, which you can't do. Unless, of course, you manufacture evidence and lie.

And that, too, will put you in a cell. There's this thing called perjury. Judges don't like it. Don't like having their time wasted. Think about it, Simeon. Think about your wife and your kids." David waved his hand. "About your employment potential."

A woman entered the open area from the hallway, nodding at him as she passed. Simeon faked a decent smile for the woman's benefit, then slid a hard look to David. "We're done. Get out."

Gladly. "Sure. But be smart. Whoever you're working for, his name isn't on the complaint against Amanda. Yours is. And your life could go down the toilet because of it."

"Get. Out."

"Be smart, Simeon. Do the right thing."

On his way out the door, David's phone rang. Penny. Huh. Her two-point-five hours of cooldown must have ended early. That or their mother had gotten to her. He hit the button. "Hey. I was going to call you about before."

"Hi," she said, her voice breathy and rushed.

He pushed through the door and met glaring sunshine. He patted his jacket pocket but remembered he'd left his sunglasses in the car. Hadn't needed them earlier. "Are you okay?"

"Yes. Jenna just called me. She talked to the lab. We got a hit on the fingerprints from that key."

Whoa. Jack. Pot. Getting a hit off the prints meant the guy was in the system. And that meant he had a criminal record. "Rap sheet?"

"No. Did you know anyone who works with children needs to be fingerprinted?"

"Yeah."

"Well, big brother, you're not going to believe where this guy works."

"Tell me."

"The Dyce Youth Center."

HAVING RECLAIMED A portion of her sanity, thanks to Lexi, Amanda marched into the youth center with her head high, her makeup and hair repaired and her one remaining completed painting ready to be shown.

Life and business as usual.

Sort of.

Mrs. Dyce couldn't know it, but this little visit would restore Amanda's sense of routine. Bring her back to the existence she'd had before David Hennings had marched through her front door and upended her life with his presence and, after last night, a few bouts of borderline rough sex she'd never before even considered participating in.

What she needed was exactly what she was about to do. Show her work, explain the details, share her love of art. This was where Amanda belonged. Where she thrived. The safe zone.

Neutral.

Forget David Hennings. The man had already torn her up in a million different ways. Why give him more opportunities?

But maybe Lexi was right and she needed to lighten up. The time with him, for the most part, had been good, extraordinary even. No one could be perfect 100 percent of the time.

"Hello, Amanda," Mrs. Dyce said, striding toward her in gray slacks and heels and a black blazer. She wore a pearl necklace and earrings, and the minimal accessories screamed elegance and class and money.

Money that would help Amanda's bank account. And, considering that her assets were currently unavailable, a fresh infusion of funds would be nice.

"Hello, Mrs. Dyce. Thank you for letting me come by."

"I should be thanking you." She gestured to the large narrow box Amanda held. "Do you need help with that?"

She gripped the handle, lifting the painting a few inches. "No. Thank you. I'm used to it."

"All right, then. We'll look at it in the conference room. There's room to spread out in there."

Amanda followed Mrs. Dyce down the same hallway she and David had traveled earlier in the week. Mrs. Dyce stopped in front of a doorway—apparently their destination—just across from her office and waved Amanda in.

Once inside the conference room, a large space with a table for ten and leather cushioned chairs, Amanda set the painting down, resting the box against the wall while she rummaged through her tote for her portable easel. In seconds, she'd have it set up and be able to show the painting on it. As much as Lexi teased her about the pop-up easel, it came in handy for displaying her work in a pinch. Except...*whoopsie*...she'd forgotten it in the trunk.

"I'm sorry. I forgot my easel in the car. It'll only take me a second to grab it. Do you mind?"

"It's not a problem at all. Go ahead. While you're doing that, I'll see if my husband is still here. I'd like him to look at the painting with me. I always prefer to get his opinion on large purchases." The older woman smiled. "Keeps things running smoothly."

After that fight with David, Amanda was beginning to learn. "I know exactly what you mean." She held her finger up. "I'll be back in a flash."

She walked down the hallway to the door she'd entered from. The parking lot behind the building, a definite perk in Chicago, made for easy access. She popped her trunk, found the easel and headed back inside. As she climbed the brick steps, a man exiting the building pushed the door open and held it for her.

She glanced up to offer a smile and thanks and stared into the face of the man who'd stolen the skull.

Chapter Thirteen

Amanda stood on the step, unmoving, for a solid five seconds, maybe more, before her brain clicked. When it finally did, she whipped around, ready to run, but he clamped on to her arm.

"No," he said.

And the deep, shaky voice came back to her. *I don't want to hurt you.* She tugged, but his hand tightened and he stepped back, dragging her up the steps as she threw her weight into her heels, resisting momentum. *Useless.* The man outweighed her by at least one hundred pounds.

"Help!"

Someone had to be nearby. In the parking lot, walking the street, anywhere. She swung her head around. "Help!"

Nothing. Not a pedestrian in sight.

The man yanked and a blast of pain shot up her arm into her shoulder. He knew he had her. She kicked out, but he leaped just out of her reach. Missed.

"Oh, my God."

Amanda peered over his shoulder and spotted Mrs. Dyce holding the door partway open. Finally, someone to help.

"Call the police," Amanda said. "This man broke into David's apartment. He stole the skull I was working on."

Still holding her, the man angled back and his grip

slipped. Amanda yanked and—*yes*—freedom. She spun back to the door, sprinted toward it, made it four steps until he caught her and latched on to the back of her jacket.

"Stay still!" he hollered.

"Sssshhh!" Mrs. Dyce hissed. "Get her in here."

The words jabbed at Amanda, tiny swords stabbing at her ears, forcing their way in, but…what? She didn't understand. "I don't…"

What was happening?

But the man tugged her backward, dragging her down the hall, and Amanda started screaming. Two, maybe three seconds passed and the man's meaty hand clamped over her mouth. Still, Amanda screamed. The sound was muffled but at least it was there as the man hauled her across the tiled floor, her feet skidding, failing to gain traction.

He shoved her back into the conference room, where her painting still lay against the wall.

What's happening?

Without breaking stride, Mrs. Dyce closed the door, and the icy control in which she did it made Amanda shiver. Where was the caring, loving woman who'd helped the masses?

Slowly, she turned to the man, her cheeks sucked in, her eyes more than a little wild. But the control remained. Demented calm, that was what this was.

She moved closer to him, a few steps away. "How could you be so *stupid*?"

In minutes she'd transformed from pleasant and elegant to mean and scrappy. Unhinged.

"I don't understand," Amanda said.

"Shut up! You—" she poked at the man "—find my husband. Get him in here. *Now*."

The man scurried from the room, closing the door behind him.

Disbelief consumed Amanda. "What are you *doing*?"

Insanity. All of it.

"Stop talking, Amanda. Before you get hurt."

The entire episode was bizarre. *What's she doing?* And then the pieces, albeit odd pieces, started to merge. The visit to the center, chatting with Mrs. Dyce about the reconstruction and agreeing to work with the detective, all of it had been discussed. With a woman who had massive connections within the city.

But what did the reconstruction have to do with the Dyces? "You knew that man stole the skull? David almost got hurt!"

"Shut up. I tried to stop you. I tried. All I wanted was for you to go away. To give up on this *reconstruction*. And now look what you've done."

Amanda shook her head, disbelief stunting her thoughts. There'd be time for figuring it all out later. She eyed the door, but Mrs. Dyce stood in her path. *Get around her.* The woman had twenty-five years on her. If Amanda could get close enough, she'd shove her and maybe escape.

"You'll never get by me. Believe me. I'm not willing to let meaningless people destroy my life."

The door came open and a tall man with dark hair, graying at the temples, stepped in, his large frame filling the doorway. She'd seen Mr. Dyce on television plenty of times, but he appeared bigger now, more confident. Behind him was the other man. The messenger boy.

"That idiot!" Mrs. Dyce poked her finger. "He walked out when she was here. How *stupid*!"

"You witch!" the man said to her. "After what I've done for you?"

Mr. Dyce glanced at Amanda, his eyes darting. The

confidence from seconds ago slid away and his body became more erect, his movements jerky. He'd just been appointed to a presidential committee, an honor men in his position rarely saw, and his wife was detaining someone against her will.

"You have to let me go," Amanda said. "Whatever this is, holding me will only get worse for you."

"Stop talking," Mrs. Dyce said.

"No. You two are beloved in this city. After this, you're done. It's over. Tell her to let me go."

But Mr. Dyce's eyes were still bouncing around, that panic shredding him. "Scott, leave us," he said.

Scott, the lackey, slid his gaze to Amanda, then back to Mr. Dyce. "Whatever happens, I'm not going down for this."

"Oh, shut up!" Mrs. Dyce hissed.

"Shut up? I've been helping you this whole time."

"Just let me go," Amanda said, still not sure what exactly they were talking about. "I'll walk out and everyone is safe."

"Irene," Mr. Dyce said to his wife. "What are we doing? This is crazy."

The woman's eyes got huge. The kind of look fueled by rage and torment. "What are we doing? We're saving your career. *We* need to stay together on this."

"Yes. We do. But I just talked to Simeon. He's out. This plan of yours has gone too far. It needs to stop."

Simeon. What had she gotten into with these people?

"Wonderful," Mrs. Dyce said, sarcasm oozing. "What do you propose?" She pointed at Amanda. "She can send us all to prison. She has to go."

"No. She doesn't. Accidentally killing a homeless person is one thing. This? This is murder and I won't do it."

"Isn't this typical? Once again, on my own."

"Stop it."

"No. I was afraid that night and you were gone. You're always tending to someone *else's* problems. If you'd been available, this would have wound up differently." She held her hands out. "I had to protect myself and now we're almost there. Please. We'll just make her go away."

No. *No, no, no.* "David knows I'm here."

Mrs. Dyce marched to the credenza, where a brass sculpture of two children playing sat on the top. She picked it up, checked its weight and looked back at Amanda with that same menacing face from minutes ago. "Well, that's too bad for him, then, isn't it?"

The man—Scott—backed toward the door. "Lady, you are insane. I'm out. I was willing to help you six years ago, but now you two are on your own."

He slipped from the room.

"Irene," Mr. Dyce said, giving his back to Amanda.

Go! With the couple occupied, she ran. Bolted to the door, grabbed the handle and yanked. The door came halfway open. Freedom. *Run.*

Clunk.

A huge weight blasted the side of her head and she stared at the hallway, at her chance to escape, at freedom.

At least until it went black.

DAVID CHARGED THROUGH the back entrance of the youth center and scanned the doors on either side of the long hallway. A man strode toward him, a big guy in ratty khakis who looked…familiar.

Him. The guy he had chased out of the condo.

David kept moving, heading straight for the man, until something in his face changed. Recognition.

The man slowed, but David ignored him—*wait for it*—and moved just past him. The guy, thinking he'd dodged one, kept his gaze glued to the door, but David whirled and slammed him with a fist behind the ear.

Boom.

He hit the floor.

What most people didn't realize, and David learned while working out with a buddy who was into Ultimate Fighting, was that a well-aimed punch to the temple or behind the ear would drop someone. Immediately.

Case in point: the unconscious man at his feet. Hearing a commotion from behind one of the doors, he hustled to it. Muffled, hissing voices came from the other side and he halted, listened for a second. *Idiot...your career... you did this.*

Gently, he turned the knob and suddenly the door flew open, smacking against the interior wall. He flinched at the bang, but his eyes fixed on something.

A body. On the floor.

Amanda.

She lay unconscious, arms and legs sprawled at her sides while blood seeped from her head, and something inside him went berserk. Just blew his mind.

Mrs. Dyce stood over Amanda, fiercely gripping a sculpture. She directed her hard, almost desperate gaze at David. "She attacked us!"

Liar. All David was sure of was one of them—most likely Mrs. Dyce—had knocked Amanda out cold. And that was a problem. For them.

"Irene, shut up." Mr. Dyce's voice climbed an octave higher than his normal calm baritone.

David shifted his gaze between them. First he'd have to take out Mr. Dyce. He was the bigger, more powerful opponent. By then, McCall would be showing up to question Mrs. Dyce about the employee who'd broken into David's condo. When he arrived, he'd find a whole lot more than that. Between the two of them, they'd get this under control.

Lunging left, David drove his shoulder into his best friend's father's gut, propelling the man backward, off his feet, both of them crashing to the floor. They landed hard, David on top as air whooshed from Mr. Dyce. Behind him, Mrs. Dyce wailed at him to stop and Mr. Dyce started swinging, the punches missing their mark and sliding off David's arms and shoulders and the side of his head. David reared up, jabbed once, twice and the final time landed a cross on the jaw. Mr. Dyce groaned, a low guttural sound, and his eyes rolled back.

Mrs. Dyce. *Where is she?* David leaped to his feet and twisted in time to see her, on the move, a foot from him, sculpture in hand. He dodged left, ducking under her arms as she raised the sculpture. Before she could clock him, he shoved her, knocking her off balance, and she cried out, tipping forward until she dropped across her husband's legs, the sculpture still in her hand. She kicked out and swung the heavy piece, but the weight and her weird angle made her efforts useless. She swung wide. *Missed.* Breaths coming fast, he reached down, gripped her wrist and squeezed until she winced. She opened her hand and the sculpture fell. It thunked against the carpeted floor, and the thought of Amanda getting hit with that thing made his stomach flip.

He shoved Mrs. Dyce away, grabbed the sculpture with one hand and wrapped his fingers around the solid base. Not all that heavy—for him—but enough to split someone's head. At his feet, Mrs. Dyce began to sob. The wailing hit him wrong. Forget empathy or sadness for a woman he'd known most of his life. Those tears were tiny shards of glass scraping against him. Behind him, Amanda groaned and relief gripped him. At least she was still alive. Whatever Mrs. Dyce had to say, he wasn't interested. He shook the statue at her.

"Move and I'll crack *your* skull with it."

DAVID SWUNG AROUND the corner of the hospital hallway on his way to Amanda's room and received one hell of a shock.

He stopped short and cocked his head, wondering just what the next thirty seconds would bring.

Leaning against the wall outside Amanda's room—at least he assumed it was Amanda's room because why else would Penny be standing there?—his sister fiddled with her phone. Probably answering emails.

He started toward her and she glanced up. Spotting him, she tucked her phone away and stood tall.

If she was readying for a fight, he didn't have it in him. He'd been at the PD giving his statement, damned near frantic wondering how badly Amanda had been hurt. She'd regained consciousness, but they'd hauled her off to the hospital straightaway and no one had given him any updates on her condition.

"Hi," she said, nodding toward the door. "The doctor is in with her. She was kind of worked up, so they gave her something to settle her down. The doctor said she has a concussion but thankfully no fractures. There's a deep cut that they put staples in. Blech. Literally, she has staples in her head. They had to shave the area, and let me tell you, when she comes out of her fog, she is not going to be happy about her funky new hairdo."

"Oh, man. But no fractures. That's great."

"They want to keep her overnight, but the doctor thinks she can go home tomorrow."

David nodded, taking a second to absorb the relief bullying its way through the massive tension in his neck.

Crazy few days. And even with McCall sorting through the mess David had left at the police station, he still had work to do regarding his sister.

"Pen, what are you doing here?"

She shrugged. "After you called Dad, he told me you were giving a statement and I wasn't sure if Amanda was alone. I just didn't want her to be by herself while you were tied up."

On his way to the police station, he'd called his father and asked him to meet him there just in case that key he'd swiped came back on him. Which, so far, it hadn't, but man, oh, man, his sister had done this for a woman she barely knew. And he hadn't even asked.

"Thank you for doing that for her."

"You're welcome."

But after she said that she shook her head and pressed her lips together in a way that told him he'd once again screwed up. What now? He replayed the last ten seconds in his mind and it hit him. "I can see you're about to unleash on me. You don't have to. I know what I did."

"Well, *David*, you recognized the sign. That's progress at least."

He smiled. "Thank you for being here for her *and* for me. You knew I'd be worried about her being alone."

"We may not always get along, but you're my brother and I love you. You have this massive protective streak. I figured I'd sit with her until you got here."

He hugged her. Just reached across and wrapped his baby sister in a bone-crushing hug. And, lookie here, she hugged him back. Not one of those quick, barely touching hugs that had a mountain of tension. This was the real deal and something they hadn't done in years.

Still hanging on, he patted her back. "Thank you."

Penny released him.

"I'm sorry about before," he said. "And about Jenna."

"Forget it. Let's just please learn from it. I'm not always angling for a fight. Not anymore at least. A lot has changed since you've been gone. My life is different. I'm happy and intend to stay that way. I don't want to compete with you for Dad's attention."

What? He craned his neck, started to say something and stopped. "I'm confused."

"I know you think I'm a brat, but put yourself in my place for a minute. You were the one Dad wanted at the firm. You're the brilliant one. And Zac has always sort of breezed through, doing what he wanted and somehow managing not to infuriate the 'rents. After you chose not to be at the firm and he decided he wanted to be a prosecutor, the boys in the family became a nonissue. Me? I always wanted to be with Dad. Always. But, believe me, as much as Dad loves me and spoils me, he wanted one of his sons by his side. I was the runner-up. Sometimes that knowledge got the best of me. All I wanted was to prove myself and I took it out on you. I couldn't resist poking at you. I don't need to do that anymore and I'm sorry."

David ran his hand over his face. Was it tomorrow yet? Sure felt like it. The past few days had definitely taken a piece out of him and now his sister had damn near floored him with this revelation. All the fights and the vicious sarcasm and the general being a pain in the rear to each other and it came down to one issue. Pretty much the same issue for each of them. David had always resented being the outsider.

And so did Penny.

"Pen, I'm sorry. I never knew. Really, even if I had thought about it, I'm not sure I'd have figured out you were trying to break into the boys' club."

He'd been so wrapped up in his own life, he'd never

considered what went on in Penny's life. Or even Zac's. But Zac was…Zac. Nobody worried about him.

"You didn't know and I never told you."

"I don't want to fight anymore. I know I've said that before, but I can't do this anymore. And, listen, after the talk I had with Mom this morning, I think we've pretty much worn her out. She's about to dropkick us both."

Penny scrunched her nose. "Did she have the face? That one when she drills you with her eyes?"

"No. She had the face beyond the drilling."

"Ew."

"Yeah. Not good. She told me to take you to lunch once a week—just us—so we can get to know each other. After this conversation, that's a good idea. I'd like to get to know my sister again. And Russ. He seems like a good guy."

"He is. You two would probably get along. You're both bullheaded."

David laughed. "Harsh!"

"Oh, boohoo. As far as lunch goes, Fridays are usually good for me."

"Fridays?"

"Unless I'm in court. But I'd like to have lunch with you." She grinned, rubbing her hands together like the mischievous twelve-year-old girl she used to be. "Plus, it'll drive Zac crazy wondering what we're talking about."

Good old Penny. Always busting chops.

"Okay," he said. "Check your schedule for next Friday. Mom will go crazy. You'll get gummy bears out of it and I'll get brownies."

"Cha-ching!" they said at the same time.

"Ain't this great?"

The now-familiar voice coming from behind them

telegraphed things were anything but great. David turned to see McCall striding toward them.

"Not only do I get one Hennings," the detective said, "I get two. And both lawyers. Someone shoot me."

"Hello, Detective," Penny said. "You can't question her at the moment."

His sister. Right to lawyer mode. Gotta love her.

"Relax, Counselor. I'm here to update her."

The door to Amanda's room opened and the doctor stepped out. McCall flashed his badge.

"Hello, Detective. You can speak with her but not for too long."

"Thanks, Doc."

"We'll run a few more tests, but assuming nothing comes up, she can probably go home tomorrow. Let her rest, though. All of you."

"Sure thing, Doc." McCall said. "Thank you."

"I'll check back in a bit."

The doctor headed off and McCall jerked a thumb toward the door. "I'm guessing she won't mind you hearing, so come in and I won't have to do this twice. It's a helluva story."

AMANDA'S HEAD WAS coming apart. Well, coming apart might have been an exaggeration given the staples literally holding her skin together and the lack of a fracture—absolutely good news considering that she could be dead right now—but she definitely had pain.

The door to her room swished open and without lifting her head, she turned to see Penny enter the room followed by David and Detective McCall.

Immediately, her body craved David. Just being in the same room made her want to pull him close. Something she'd have to figure out how to deal with after the fight they'd had that morning. Who knew where they'd go from here?

She'd deal with that later. When her head wasn't coming apart.

For now, she hoped McCall had news for her. News that would inform her that she'd soon be back to some sort of routine. She didn't want to be greedy, but her routine would be the best thing for her.

She pushed herself up only to have the room spin. *That won't work.* Resting back, she felt around for the bed's remote.

"Hang on." David rushed to the side of the bed. "It's hanging off the bed. We'll wind it through the safety bars so it doesn't fall."

"Thank you."

He handed her the remote, their fingers brushing lightly. As usual, something inside her pinged. He did that to her, stirred her up, gave her a zap of something warm and hopeful, and suddenly she hated it. Twenty-four hours ago, it was a blessing she'd never experienced. Now, after her conversation with Lexi, it just confused her and she didn't know what she wanted.

Lie. She knew. She wanted him. Without the drama. The drama would decimate her. But she didn't want to be the person Lexi described her as, either. Didn't want to constantly be waiting for the next bad thing. Her mother would have expected more of her.

Slowly, she raised the bed enough that she could see but not bring a fresh bout of dizziness.

David ran his fingers over her cheek and she closed her eyes. She should pull away and not let him touch her. Touching made her feel the stupid zing and she couldn't think straight with that going on.

But just this once, after what they'd been through together, she'd let it happen. Comfort couldn't be bad.

"How's the head?" McCall asked.

"It feels like I got clubbed."

"Um," Penny said, moving to the other side of the bed. "Maybe because you did?"

McCall gestured to the gauze circling her head. "She must have whacked you good."

The staples holding her skin together proved it. Plus, she had to have part of her head shaved because the doctor, as he'd said, wanted better visualization. So, along with the injury, she'd look like a freak.

Bigger things to worry about.

For now, she'd stay grateful for the fact that she wasn't in the morgue. But that damned woman had inflicted a lot of damage to her life and when the medication wore off, Amanda suspected she'd be spitting nails.

Be grateful.

She sighed as McCall stepped up to the end of the bed. As much as she didn't want to discuss the incident, the detective was obviously here for a statement. And she'd give it to him. If for no other reason than to help him solve his case. All she'd been able to assume was that the Dyces somehow knew the woman whose skull Amanda was reconstructing. They also obviously had knowledge about her death.

She met the detective's gaze. "I'll tell you what I remember."

He held his hand up. "In a minute. Let me update you."

This sounded hopeful.

"We've arrested the Dyces and Scott Bench. He's the one who stole the skull cast."

"He was the man at the youth center, too," Amanda said. "I recognized him."

"Yeah. He's also your guy from the storage unit. He'd been following you and pulled the alarm."

"Bastard."

"You could say that. After the scene in the conference room, he got scared. Figured he'd wind up the fall guy for the Dyces, so he gave us the story. He's thirty-four and he's worked at the youth center for eight years. Known the Dyces since he was in high school. He grew up in a rough neighborhood and was heading down a wrong path. Couple burglary arrests and some petty-crime stuff. His mother took him to see Reggie Dyce speak at a rally, and the kid formed a relationship with him. They helped him get his act together. A few years went by and when he got married, they hired him to do maintenance at the center."

"He felt indebted to them?"

"Oh, yeah."

David cocked his head. "How indebted?"

McCall blew out a breath. "Enough to help them bury our victim's body."

"My God," Penny said.

Amanda sighed. The world simply terrified her. These people were beloved for their charitable endeavors and their dedication to helping others. Total frauds. "What happened?"

"There's a storage shed behind the center. One night Irene finds a hammer lying around the rec room, so she takes it back to the shed. It's winter and damned cold. While she's in the shed, she hears a noise and looks up to see some girl coming at her. Irene thinks she's about to get attacked. She must have been standing in front of the door. I'm thinkin' our vic was homeless and trying to get some shelter and when Irene came into the shed, the girl tried to run. Anyways, Irene claims she got scared and swung the hammer." McCall motioned like swinging. "Tagged her good. The girl dropped like a stone."

"She was dead?"

"At the time, Irene doesn't know. But Scott Bench is putting the trash out and hears the commotion. He checks it out and finds Irene in a state of total hysterics. He gets her calmed down, but she's going on about how they'd be ruined and all their hard work wouldn't mean anything and the center would have to close. Our boy Scott realizes he has a family to support and he's got a pretty good gig at the center."

"Where was Mr. Dyce during all this?"

"At some rally downstate."

"Which is why," Amanda said, "she accused him of not being around to support her."

David shook his head. "Tell me she convinced Scott Bench to bury the body."

"This guy takes hero worship to the next level. He's a street kid. He's seen it all and he wasn't gonna risk losing his job. Or going back to life on the street. Irene panicked and begged him for help and he told her he'd take care of it. They're a rotten combination, these two. He got his brother to help him and they dealt with the body. At least until I found it while walking my dog."

Stunned, Amanda simply stared. "She killed a young woman and threw her in the trash. The woman is evil."

"Hold up," David said. "When I took Amanda to the center and asked her to pass the sketch around, it kicked this whole thing off?"

Amanda grabbed David's hand. "No. That can't be. My building was condemned before that. She must have gotten her husband to reach out to someone at City Hall. But how did she know I'd agreed to help?"

"Wait," Penny said. "At dinner the other night Mom

said she talked to Irene. When she cornered you into telling Dad you'd help. This is *Mom's* fault!"

"No," Amanda said. "It's not. It's Irene Dyce's fault." She squeezed David's hand. "The conversation with your mom probably confirmed I was involved, but remember when we saw her at the center that first time and showed her the sketch?"

"What about it?"

"She commented on the detail. I bet she recognized her."

David dropped his chin to his chest and pounded on his head with his free hand. "You're right. Babe, I'm so sorry."

But Penny waved her hand. "Just knock that off. This was *not* your fault or Mom's. The woman is nuts. After Mom told her about the reconstruction, she was coming after Amanda anyway." She winced and turned to Amanda. "That sounded harsh. I'm sorry. I don't want him thinking this is his fault. My mother was already working the Dyces for their help on this."

"I know," Amanda said. "But what about Simeon Davis? Before Mrs. Dyce hit me, I heard Mr. Dyce tell her Simeon had backed out. What was that about?"

"Yeah. He got friendly with the Dyces after doing volunteer work for them, and when Simeon had trouble finding work, Reggie got the guy a job at the insurance agency. He was about to lose his house, so that job saved his butt."

"I don't understand how he knows me," Amanda said.

"He doesn't. The Dyces are in bed with the state's attorney. They helped get her elected. When you signed on to do the reconstruction, they made up some bull story about one of their volunteers being a victim of a check-cashing scheme and warned the SA she should look into it. They fed Simeon some line about wanting to make sure no other people got defrauded and asked Simeon to back them up. Make it look like more than one person got scammed. He did it."

"Because he owed them."

"Listen, this guy isn't the sharpest knife in the drawer. He took pride in the fact that Dyce came to him. He wanted to be the hero. Anyway, he went along with it."

David knocked his knuckles against the rail of the bed. "That's why the SA went into court saying if the assets weren't preserved, Amanda would deplete them before an investigation could be launched. Except, I went to Simeon and scared the hell out of him."

"Yes, Counselor, and thank you, but we're gonna talk about you butting into my investigation. Again."

"It's bizarre," Amanda said. "The lengths they were willing to go to."

"Yes, it is," Penny said. "But they've worked for years to reach a certain level. Mr. Dyce has just been appointed to a presidential committee. It's the pinnacle for him."

David huffed. "They wouldn't give up that status. People are so damned twisted."

"Yeah, well." McCall waggled his fingers. "I have the icing on this cake for you."

Exhausted, Amanda put her hands up. "Detective, I'm not sure I can take much more."

"You're gonna have to because we got a hit on your sketch. One of the syndicated crime shows ran it last night and someone thought she looked like the daughter of a neighbor. They called the neighbor and told them to check out the sketch online."

A hit. Just off the sketch. If it panned out, they'd have identified the victim before the reconstruction was even complete. *Don't.* Getting excited before they had a positive identification would be reckless. An emotional risk. So what? She could be hopeful. That was what she'd call it. Hope.

"Was it her?"

"It's close enough that we're getting DNA to be sure. She was a runaway. Been gone a couple of years and they'd lost touch with her. They didn't know where she was, never mind dead. That's all I got now."

McCall's cell phone beeped and he pulled it from his pocket. He read something on it and stowed the phone again. "Damn. I gotta go. I'll be back in a while to get a statement from you. All right?"

"That's fine. Thank you, Detective. This is great news. Sad, but great, too."

He set his hand on the blanket over her foot and squeezed. "It is good news. And thank you. If the DNA matches, you brought this girl home."

Chapter Fourteen

After McCall left, Penny made a performance out of checking her watch and announcing she had just a *ton* of work to do. The ton of work must have magically appeared after David, rather violently, jerked his head toward the door.

This family. Completely nuts.

But they were funny, too. And caring.

"So," Penny chirped. "I will see you both later. Call if you need something. Toodles."

Finger waving as she went, she fast-walked toward the door, something Amanda noticed earlier also. Penny fast-walked everywhere.

"She's a ball of energy, huh?"

"You could say that. It's her Napoleon complex. She's tiny, but she's deadly."

"You should make up with her."

David tugged gently on the hair poking from under Amanda's bandage. "I already have. Right outside this room. I showed up when the doctor was in here and I cornered her. Turns out, my sister and I have a few things in common. We're going to lunch together next week to discuss them."

"Really?"

"You don't believe me?"

"I absolutely believe you. I'm just surprised."

"I had a talk with my mother this morning after I infuriated everyone and generally made a jerk out of myself. Turns out, my mother is fed up with Penny and me fighting all the time. She came up with the lunch idea. It's a pretty good one. It'll give me a chance to get to know my sister again. Heck, maybe it'll be a weekly thing."

"I'm glad, David."

"Me, too." He glanced down at the safety rail. "Can I lower this?"

"Sure."

He lowered the rail and perched on the edge of the bed, his weight sinking the one side a bit. *Too close.* He should go. Let her be for a while. The doctor said she needed rest. And she should inform him that the closeness confused her, made her crave time alone to sort out her feelings. She should tell him.

Absolutely.

And yet she sat with her mouth closed and her thoughts flying.

"Is this okay?" he asked.

"Sure."

Again with the "sure"? That word needed to be banished. Forever. No. Not okay. That was what she *should* have said. Just thrown him out of here. Instead, he was sitting on her bed, way too close, and already she knew her life would never be what it had been. How could it be after all this? And maybe that was the point. That life meant bumps and bends and hills to be conquered.

None of which could be accomplished in neutral.

"Amanda, I'm sorry. For everything. For getting you into this mess, for tearing your life up and for blaming you this morning. No excuses. I'm an idiot sometimes."

Oh, she might love this man.

She bit her bottom lip but finally gave up and smiled. “You’re funny, David.”

“Sometimes I’m that, too.” He shifted a little, facing her straight on, his soul-piercing gaze glued to hers. “Will you let me try to fix this? This week has been hell, straight up hell, but I knew we’d get through it. I knew. But when you walked out this morning, that did me in. I was mad and hurt and irritated at myself and everyone else. And then my mother got a hold of me.”

Amanda laughed. “Poor baby.”

He grinned at her. “Seriously, she’s tough. And most of the time, she’s right. Annoying, that. Since I’m coming clean, I might as well tell you that she has you lined up to be the next member of our family.”

Gulp. “Wow.”

David set his giant hand on hers, and his palm was warm as he curled his fingers around hers, cocooning her. She rested her head back and closed her eyes because this was the part of being with David she loved. That feeling of safety and warmth. With that, though, came the risk of heartbreak. *No neutral.*

Not with this man.

“Yeah. No pressure there. I think she has a point, though. When I’m not being a dope we’re good together. I love talking to you and touching you. The minute you leave me, I want you back. And for a guy who spent years running, that’s new. I like it. It makes me feel…lighter. Like dealing with my crazy family isn’t so hard because I have you to make me laugh. To tell me when I’m wrong and not have it be a power struggle. To make me understand that it’s okay to disagree and it doesn’t mean you don’t support me. I get that now. This morning, my emotions took over. I’m sorry. I can’t promise my emotions won't get in the way again, but I won't blame you for it if they do. Never again."

"David—"

He raised his hand. "All I want is dinner. When all this gets hashed out, let me take you to dinner. We'll start again. Two people who've just met." He squeezed her hand. "Think about it. Please."

He stood, then raised the safety bar again. "Now I'm leaving because the doc said you need rest and they're gonna throw me out anyway." He kissed her lightly on the head, and his scent, the musky maleness she'd grown used to, surrounded her. He lingered for a few seconds before backing away. "I'll call you tomorrow."

Stop him. "Okay."

Then he turned and headed for the door. *Stop him.* But if she did, there'd be no neutral. If nothing else, he deserved better than that. Everyone did.

Even her.

"David?"

He stopped and tilted his head to the ceiling but didn't turn around.

"Yes. To dinner. And, if you're not in a rush, maybe you could sit with me for a while?"

He turned and strode toward her and instinctively she sat up. The room spun and she gripped the sheet, waiting for him to reach her again, and there he was, instantly by her side, leaning over the rail. But as fast as he was moving, he gently cupped her face in his giant hands and kissed her, a long, slow kiss that she wasn't sure she could ever live without again. Kisses from David were either fast and fierce or slow and gentle, each one different and surprising and perfect. This would be life with him. Different. Surprising. Perfect.

And definitely not in neutral.

Chapter Fifteen

One Month Later

David eased his car to a stop in front of a bungalow in Ina, Illinois, a small town almost five hours south of Chicago consisting of a whopping two and a half square miles. Amanda studied the gutter hanging from one side of the tiny house and the ripped screens on the two front windows. With a little work—maybe more than a little—the house could be adorable.

From what Amanda knew, nothing that had gone on in this house, not one single thing, could ever be considered adorable. This had been the home of Juliette Powers, the nineteen-year-old woman whose reconstruction sat in a box on the floor of David's backseat.

"This is it," David said.

"I see that."

Yearning for freedom and a better life, Juliette had run from this house at sixteen. Her mother's second husband had been abusive and getting nastier by the second, and Juliette had craved independence and a life free of yelling and fists. She'd been on her own, working odd jobs, living in shelters, for almost three years before her death.

Why she was in that storage shed the night she died, no one would ever truly know, but Amanda suspected Detective McCall's theory—that the young woman needed a place to hunker down on a cold night—was as close as any.

David shifted the car into Park and shut the engine. "You ready for this?"

She nodded. "I am. I didn't think I would be, but it feels…right. Juliette didn't get a happy ending, but we brought her home. That's what I'm hanging on to. She's safe now."

Three weeks earlier, David and Amanda, along with Detective McCall, had brought Juliette's remains—her skull and the hair found near it—home and attended her funeral. Now they were back. All because Amanda wanted Juliette to be remembered as a beautiful young woman, so she had finished her reconstruction on the second duplicate skull cast the lab had provided her. Scott Bench had disposed of the first one by tossing it off a bridge into the Chicago River. So many times, they'd tried to dump Juliette, to make it that she'd never be identified, but somehow, she refused to go unnoticed.

"I don't want this to sound condescending," David said, "but I'm proud of you. You've done an amazing thing here."

Amanda shrugged. "You helped. But thank you. I can't say I'm happy about it, but there's satisfaction in knowing who she was. Giving her a name again. We did that, David. Together."

"I know."

He leaned over the console and kissed her. Just a soft peck before backing away half an inch. She opened her eyes and met his alluring blue gaze that never failed to spark energy in her.

"I love you, David Hennings."

His eyes popped wide. He knew her well enough, more

than well enough, to know an admission like that, putting her heart out there, allowing herself to be vulnerable, didn't come easy. He had, in fact, cracked the code. By being honorable and trustworthy, he'd made it easy for her to love him. Case closed.

"Well," he said, "that's good news."

And then the idiot grinned. Just sat there with a smug smile and she wanted to throttle him. Let him have it because she'd just told him she loved him, and he wanted to tease her about it. Even so, she felt fairly confident his feelings ran as deep. The week prior he'd slipped and almost said it, but he'd stopped himself, probably afraid he'd spook her. Well, fine.

She reached to the floorboard and grabbed her purse. "I have something to show you."

"Finally a naked picture of you?"

"You wish."

She placed a folded sheet of paper into his palm and he pursed his lips.

"Go ahead," she urged. "Read it."

After opening it, he scanned it. The smile he'd just hit her with grew, and seeing it, seeing him happy and proud—of her—made something clog in her throat. She smacked her hands over her eyes before she started bawling. These past few weeks had been like this. One giant release of pent-up tears. Years' and years' worth. As healthy as it was to let all the fear and pain go, she'd prefer to ditch the waterworks. Just enjoy happiness for a change.

"The forensic workshop," he said. "You're going."

She dragged her hands down her face, then wiped them on her slacks. "I am. It starts next month. I'll be gone three weeks, but when I come back, I think I'll be ready to officially try forensic sculpting. I'm not afraid of it anymore. I'm out of neutral, David. With you, with my work, all of it. Thank you."

He leaned over the console again, wrapped his hand around the back of her head and hit her with one of his mind-melting kisses, more ardent this time, changing it up from a minute ago and reinforcing her belief that he would always offer surprises. After the years stuck in her safe zone, David had managed to pull her out of it and make her comfortable doing so.

He broke the kiss but held on. "I love you," he said. "You have to know that, right? I didn't want to rush you."

She nodded. "I do know. And thank you for not rushing me. For letting me get there on my own. I needed to say it first. With you, there's no neutral. There's just us—and your crazy family—and that's all I'll ever need."

* * * * *

Read on for a sneak preview of FATAL AFFAIR,
the first book in the FATAL *series by*
New York Times *bestselling author*
Marie Force

ONE

THE SMELL HIT him first.

"Ugh, what the hell is that?" Nick Cappuano dropped his keys into his coat pocket and stepped into the spacious, well-appointed Watergate apartment that his boss, Senator John O'Connor, had inherited from his father.

"Senator!" Nick tried to identify the foul metallic odor.

Making his way through the living room, he noticed parts and pieces of the suit John wore yesterday strewn over sofas and chairs, laying a path to the bedroom. He had called the night before to check in with Nick after a dinner meeting with Virginia's Democratic Party leadership, and said he was on his way home. Nick had reminded his thirty-six-year-old boss to set his alarm.

"Senator?" John hated when Nick called him that when they were alone, but Nick insisted the people in John's life afford him the respect of his title.

The odd stench permeating the apartment caused a tingle of anxiety to register on the back of Nick's neck. "John?"

He stepped into the bedroom and gasped. Drenched in blood, John sat up in bed, his eyes open but vacant. A knife spiked through his neck held him in place against the headboard. His hands rested in a pool of blood in his lap.

Gagging, the last thing Nick noticed before he bolted to the bathroom to vomit was that something was hanging out of John's mouth.

Once the violent retching finally stopped, Nick stood up on shaky legs, wiped his mouth with the back of his hand, and rested against the vanity, waiting to see if there would be more. His cell phone rang. When he didn't take the call, his pager vibrated. Nick couldn't find the wherewithal to answer, to say the words that would change everything. *The senator is dead. John's been murdered.* He wanted to go back to when he was still in his car, fuming and under the assumption that his biggest problem that day would be what to do about the man-child he worked for who had once again slept through his alarm.

Thoughts of John, dating back to their first meeting in a history class at Harvard freshman year, flashed through Nick's mind, hundreds of snippets spanning a nearly twenty-year friendship. As if to convince himself that his eyes had not deceived him, he leaned forward to glance into the bedroom, wincing at the sight of his best friend—the brother of his heart—stabbed through the neck and covered with blood.

Nick's eyes burned with tears, but he refused to give in to them. Not now. Later maybe, but not now. His phone rang again. This time he reached for it and saw it was Christina, his deputy chief of staff, but didn't take the call. Instead, he dialed 911.

Taking a deep breath to calm his racing heart and making a supreme effort to keep the hysteria out of his voice, he said, "I need to report a murder." He gave the address and stumbled into the living room to wait for the police, all the while trying to get his head around the image of his dead friend, a visual he already knew would haunt him forever.

Twenty long minutes later, two officers arrived, took a quick look in the bedroom and radioed for backup. Nick was certain neither of them recognized the victim.

He felt as if he was being sucked into a riptide, pulled further and further from the safety of shore, until drawing a breath became a laborious effort. He told the cops exactly what happened—his boss failed to show up for work, he came looking for him and found him dead.

"Your boss's name?"

"United States Senator John O'Connor." Nick watched the two young officers go pale in the instant before they made a second more urgent call for backup.

"Another scandal at the Watergate," Nick heard one of them mutter.

His cell phone rang yet again. This time he reached for it.

"Yeah," he said softly.

"Nick!" Christina cried. "Where the *hell* are you guys? Trevor's having a heart attack!" She referred to their communications director, who had back-to-back interviews scheduled for the senator that morning.

"He's dead, Chris."

"Who's dead? What're you talking about?"

"John."

Her soft cry broke his heart. *"No."* That she was desperately in love with John was no secret to Nick. That she was also a consummate professional who would never act on those feelings was one of the many reasons Nick respected her.

"I'm sorry to just blurt it out like that."

"How?" she asked in a small voice.

"Stabbed in his bed."

Her ravaged moan echoed through the phone. "But who… I mean, *why*?"

"The cops are here, but I don't know anything yet. I need you to request a postponement on the vote."

"I can't," she said, adding in a whisper, "I can't think about that right now."

"You have to, Chris. That bill is his legacy. We can't let all his hard work be for nothing. Can you do it? For him?"

"Yes...okay."

"You have to pull yourself together for the staff, but don't tell them yet. Not until his parents are notified."

"Oh, God, his poor parents. You should go, Nick. It'd be better coming from you than cops they don't know."

"I don't know if I can. How do I tell people I love that their son's been murdered?"

"He'd want it to come from you."

"I suppose you're right. I'll see if the cops will let me."

"What're we going to do without him, Nick?" She posed a question he'd been grappling with himself. "I just can't imagine this world, this *life*, without him."

"I can't either," Nick said, knowing it would be a much different life without John O'Connor at the center of it.

"He's really dead?" she asked as if to convince herself it wasn't a cruel joke. "Someone killed him?"

"Yes."

OUTSIDE THE CHIEF'S office suite, Detective Sergeant Sam Holland smoothed her hands over the toffee-colored hair she corralled into a clip for work, pinched some color into cheeks that hadn't seen the light of day in weeks, and adjusted her gray suit jacket over a red scoop-neck top.

Taking a deep breath to calm her nerves and settle her chronically upset stomach, she pushed open the door and stepped inside. Chief Farnsworth's receptionist greeted her with a smile. "Go right in, Sergeant Holland. He's waiting for you."

Great, Sam thought as she left the receptionist with a weak smile. Before she could give in to the urge to turn tail and run, she erased the grimace from her face and went in.

"Sergeant." The chief, a man she'd once called Uncle Joe, stood up and came around the big desk to greet her with a firm handshake. His gray eyes skirted over her with concern and sympathy, both of which were new since "the incident." She despised being the reason for either. "You look well."

"I feel well."

"Glad to hear it." He gestured for her to have a seat. "Coffee?"

"No, thanks."

Pouring himself a cup, he glanced over his shoulder. "I've been worried about you, Sam."

"I'm sorry for causing you worry and for disgracing the department." This was the first chance she'd had to speak directly to him since she returned from a month of administrative leave, during which she'd practiced the sentence over and over. She thought she'd delivered it with convincing sincerity.

"Sam," he sighed as he sat across from her, cradling his mug between big hands. "You've done nothing to disgrace yourself or the department. Everyone makes mistakes."

"Not everyone makes mistakes that result in a dead child, Chief."

He studied her for a long, intense moment as if he was making some sort of decision. "Senator John O'Connor was found murdered in his apartment this morning."

"Jesus," she gasped. "How?"

"I don't have all the details, but from what I've been told so far, it appears he was dismembered and stabbed through the neck. Apparently, his chief of staff found him."

"Nick," she said softly.

"Excuse me?"

"Nick Cappuano is O'Connor's chief of staff."

"You know him?"

"*Knew* him. Years ago," she added, surprised and unsettled to discover the memory of him still had power over her, that just the sound of his name rolling off her lips could make her heart race.

"I'm assigning the case to you."

Surprised at being thrust so forcefully back into the real work she had craved since her return to duty, she couldn't help but ask, "Why me?"

"Because you need this, and so do I. We both need a win."

The press had been relentless in its criticism of him, of her, of the department, but to hear him acknowledge it made her ache. Her father had come up through the ranks with Farnsworth, which was probably the number one reason why she still had a job. "Is this a test? Find out who killed the senator and my previous sins are forgiven?"

He put down his coffee cup and leaned forward, elbows resting on knees. "The only person who needs to forgive you, Sam, is you."

Infuriated by the surge of emotion brought on by his softly spoken words, Sam cleared her throat and stood up. "Where does O'Connor live?"

"The Watergate. Two uniforms are already there. Crime scene is on its way." He handed her a slip of paper with the address. "I don't have to tell you that this needs to be handled with the utmost discretion."

He also didn't have to tell her that this was the only chance she'd get at redemption.

"Won't the Feds want in on this?"

"They might, but they don't have jurisdiction, and they know it. They'll be breathing down my neck, though, so report directly to me. I want to know everything ten minutes after you do. I'll smooth it with Stahl," he added, referring to the lieutenant she usually answered to.

Heading for the door, she said, "I won't let you down."

"You never have before."

With her hand resting on the door handle, she turned back to him. "Are you saying that as the chief of police or as my Uncle Joe?"

His face lifted into a small but sincere smile. "Both."

TWO

Sitting on John's sofa under the watchful eyes of the two policemen, Nick's mind raced with the staggering number of things that needed to be done, details to be seen to, people to call. His cell phone rang relentlessly, but he ignored it after deciding he would talk to no one until he had seen John's parents. Almost twenty years ago they took an instant shine to the hard-luck scholarship student their son brought home from Harvard for a weekend visit and made him part of their family. Nick owed them so much, not the least of which was hearing the news of their son's death from him if possible.

He ran his hand through his hair. "How much longer?"

"Detectives are on their way."

Ten minutes later, Nick heard her before he saw her. A flurry of activity and a burst of energy preceded the detectives' entrance into the apartment. He suppressed a groan. *Wasn't it enough that his friend and boss had been murdered? He had to face* her, *too? Weren't there thousands of District cops? Was she really the only one available?*

Sam came into the apartment, oozing authority and competence. In light of her recent troubles, Nick couldn't believe she had any of either left. "Get some tape across that door," she ordered one of the officers. "Start a log with a timeline of who got here when. No one comes in or goes out without my okay, got it?"

"Yes, ma'am. The Patrol sergeant is on his way along

with Deputy Chief Conklin and Detective Captain Malone."

"Let me know when they get here." Without so much as a glance in his direction, Nick watched her stalk through the apartment and disappear into the bedroom. Following her, a handsome young detective with bed head nodded to Nick.

He heard the murmur of voices from the bedroom and saw a camera flash. They emerged fifteen minutes later, both noticeably paler. For some reason, Nick was gratified to know the detectives working the case weren't so jaded as to be unaffected by what they'd just seen.

"Start a canvass of the building," Sam ordered her partner. "Where the hell is Crime Scene?"

"Hung up at another homicide," one of the other officers replied.

She finally turned to Nick, nothing in her pale blue eyes indicating that she recognized or remembered him. But the fact that she didn't introduce herself or ask for his name told him she knew exactly who he was. "We'll need your prints."

"They're on file," he mumbled. "Congressional background check."

She wrote something in the small notebook she tugged from the back pocket of gray, form-fitting pants. There were years on her gorgeous face that hadn't been there the last time he'd had the opportunity to look closely, and he couldn't tell if her hair was as long as it used to be since it was twisted into a clip. The curvy body and endless legs hadn't changed at all.

"No forced entry," she noted. "Who has a key?"

"Who *doesn't* have a key?"

"I'll need a list. You have a key, I assume."

Nick nodded. "That's how I got in."

"Was he seeing anyone?"

"No one serious, but he had no trouble attracting female companionship." Nick didn't add that John's casual approach to women and sex had been a source of tension between the two men, with Nick fearful that John's social life would one day lead to political trouble. He hadn't imagined it might also lead to murder.

"When was the last time you saw him?"

"When he left the office for a dinner meeting with the Virginia Democrats last night. Around six-thirty or so."

"Spoke to him?"

"Around ten when he said he was on his way home."

"Alone?"

"He didn't say, and I didn't ask."

"Take me through what happened this morning."

He told her about Christina trying to reach John, beginning at seven, and of coming to the apartment expecting to find the senator once again sleeping through his alarm.

"So this has happened before?"

"No, he's never been murdered before."

Her expression was anything but amused. "Do you think this is funny, Mr. Cappuano?"

"Hardly. My best friend is dead, Sergeant. A United States senator has been murdered. There's nothing funny about that."

"Which is why you need to answer the questions and save the droll humor for a more appropriate time."

Chastened, Nick said, "He slept through his alarm and ringing telephones at least once, if not twice, a month."

"Did he drink?"

"Socially, but I rarely saw him drunk."

"Prescription drugs? Sleeping pills?"

Nick shook his head. "He was just a very heavy sleeper."

"And it fell to his chief of staff to wake him up? There wasn't anyone else you could send?"

"The senator valued his privacy. There've been occasions when he wasn't alone, and neither of us felt his love life should be the business of his staff."

"But he didn't care if you knew who he was sleeping with?"

"He knew he could count on my discretion." He looked up, unprepared for the punch to the gut that occurred when his eyes met hers. Her unsettled expression made him wonder if she felt it, too. "His parents need to be notified. I'd like to be the one to tell them."

Sam studied him for a long moment. "I'll arrange it. Where are they?"

"At their farm in Leesburg. It needs to be soon. We're postponing a vote we worked for months to get to. It'll be all over the news that something's up."

"What's the vote for?"

He told her about the landmark immigration bill and John's role as the co-sponsor.

With a curt nod, she walked away.

An hour later, Nick was a passenger in an unmarked Metropolitan Police SUV, headed west to Leesburg with Sam at the wheel. She'd left her partner with a staggering list of instructions and insisted on accompanying Nick to tell John's parents.

"Do you need something to eat?"

He shook his head. No way could he even think about eating—not with the horrific task he had ahead of him.

Besides, his stomach hadn't recovered from the earlier bout of vomiting.

"You know, we could still call the Loudoun County Police or the Virginia State Police to handle this," she said for the second time.

"No."

After an awkward silence, she said, "I'm sorry this happened to your friend and that you had to see him that way."

"Thank you."

"Are you going to answer that?" she asked of his relentless cell phone.

"No."

"How about you turn it off then? I can't stand listening to a ringing phone."

Reaching for his belt, he grabbed his cell phone, his emotions still raw after watching John be taken from his apartment in a body bag. Before he shut the cell phone off, he called Christina.

"Hey," she said, her voice heavy with relief and emotion. "I've been trying to reach you."

"Sorry." Pulling his tie loose and releasing his top button, he cast a sideways glance at Sam, whose warm, feminine fragrance had overtaken the small space inside the car. "I was dealing with cops."

"Where are you now?"

"On my way to Leesburg."

"God," Christina sighed. "I don't envy you that. Are you okay?"

"Never better."

"I'm sorry. Dumb question."

"It's okay. Who knows what we're supposed to say or do in this situation. Did you postpone the vote?"

"Yes, but Martin and McDougal are having an apoplexy," she said, meaning John's co-sponsor on the bill and the Democratic majority leader. "They're demanding to know what's going on."

"Hold them off. Another hour. Maybe two. Same thing with the staff. I'll give you the green light as soon as I've told his parents."

"I will. Everyone knows something's up because the Capitol Police posted an officer outside John's office and won't let anyone in there."

"It's because the cops are waiting for a search warrant," Nick told her.

"Why do they need a warrant to search the victim's office?"

"Something about chain of custody with evidence and pacifying the Capitol Police."

"Oh, I see. I was thinking we should have Trevor draft a statement so we're ready."

"That's why I called."

"We'll get on it." She sounded relieved to have something to do.

"Are you okay with telling Trevor? Want me to do it?"

"I think I can do it, but thanks for asking."

"How're you holding up?" he asked.

"I'm in total shock…all that promise and potential just gone…" She began to weep again. "It's going to hurt like hell when the shock wears off."

"Yeah," he said softly. "No doubt."

"I'm here if you need anything."

"Me, too, but I'm going to shut the phone off for a while. It's been ringing nonstop."

"I'll email the statement to you when we have it done."

"Thanks, Christina. I'll call you later." Nick ended the

call and took a look at his recent email messages, hardly surprised by the outpouring of dismay and concern over the postponement of the vote. One was from Senator Martin himself—What the fuck is going on, Cappuano?

Sighing, he turned off the cell phone and dropped it into his coat pocket.

"Was that your girlfriend?" Sam asked, startling him.

"No, my deputy."

"Oh."

Wondering what she was getting at, he added, "We work closely together. We're good friends."

"Why are you being so defensive?"

"What's your *problem*?" he asked.

"I don't have a problem. You're the one with problems."

"So all that great press you've been getting lately hasn't been a problem for you?"

"Why, Nick, I didn't realize you cared."

"I don't."

"Yes, you made that very clear."

He spun halfway around in the seat to stare at her. "*Are you for real?* You're the one who didn't return any of my calls."

She glanced over at him, her face flat with surprise. "What calls?"

After staring at her in disbelief for a long moment, he settled back in his seat and fixed his eyes on the cars sharing the Interstate with them.

A few minutes passed in uneasy silence.

"What calls, Nick?"

"I called you," he said softly. "For days after that night, I tried to reach you."

"I didn't know," she stammered. "No one told me."

"It doesn't matter now. It was a long time ago." But if his reaction to seeing her again after six years of thinking about her was any indication, it *did* matter. It mattered a lot.

Continue reading Sam and Nick's story in
FATAL AFFAIR, available in
print and ebook from Carina Press.

COMING NEXT MONTH FROM

HARLEQUIN®

INTRIGUE

Available October 20, 2015

#1599 LONE WOLF LAWMAN
Appaloosa Pass Ranch • by Delores Fossen

After learning her birth father is a serial killer, rancher Addie Crockett lands in bed with Texas Ranger Weston Cade only to learn that he wants to use her as bait. Worse, Addie has no choice but to team up with Weston to protect their unborn child.

#1600 SCENE OF THE CRIME: THE DEPUTY'S PROOF
by Carla Cassidy

When Savannah Sinclair is attacked in the mysterious tunnels beneath Lost Lagoon, Deputy Josh Griffin partners with her to protect her from the dangers of deadly secrets.

#1601 CLANDESTINE CHRISTMAS
Covert Cowboys, Inc. • by Elle James

With Covert Cowboys' Kate Rivers posing as his fiancée, billionaire rancher Chase Marsden is determined to find the culprits trying to murder his old friend. But will Christmas find them under the mistletoe...or escaping kidnappers and dodging hit men?

#1602 HER UNDERCOVER DEFENDER
The Specialists: Heroes Next Door
by Debra Webb & Regan Black

Covert CIA specialist David Martin must keep a terrorist cell from using nurse Terri Barnhart as leverage to get their hands on a biotech weapon—and falling for her could compromise his mission.

#1603 SECRET AGENT SANTA
Brothers in Arms: Retribution • by Carol Ericson

When covert agent Mike Becker agrees to take on one last assignment—protecting widowed mother Claire Chadwick—he never imagines that it will turn into the opportunity to foil a terrorist attack and find redemption...

#1604 HIDDEN WITNESS
Return to Ravesville • by Beverly Long

To protect his key witness from a dangerous killer, Detective Chase Hollister will have to pose as Raney Taylor's husband. Although their wedding may have been a sham, Chase knows there's nothing fake about his feelings for Raney...

When a beautiful rancher's past threatens to take a deadly turn, her best chance of surviving is with the help of the sexy Texas Ranger she never thought she'd see again—or have to tell she's pregnant with his baby!

Read on for a sneak preview of LONE WOLF LAWMAN, the first book in USA TODAY *bestselling author* Delores Fossen*'s gripping new miniseries* ***APPALOOSA PASS RANCH.***

The silence came. Addie, staring at him. Obviously trying to make sense of this. He wanted to tell her there was nothing about this that made sense because they were dealing with a very dangerous, crazy man.

"Oh, God," she finally said.

Now, her fear was sky high, and Weston held his breath. He didn't expect Addie to go blindly along with a plan to stop her father. But she did want to stop the Moonlight Strangler from claiming another victim.

Weston was counting heavily on that.

However, Addie shook her head. "I can't help you."

That sure wasn't the reaction Weston had expected. He'd figured Addie was as desperate to end this as he was.

She squeezed her eyes shut a moment. "I'll get my mother, and we can go to the sheriff's office. Two of my brothers are there, and they can make sure this monster stays far away from us."

"You'll be safe at the sheriff's office," Weston agreed "but you can't stay there forever. Neither can your family

Eventually, you'll have to leave, and the killer will come after you."

"That can't happen!" Addie groaned and looked up at the ceiling as if she expected some kind of divine help. "I can't be in that kind of danger."

Weston tried to keep his voice as calm as possible. Hard to do, though, with the emotions swirling like a tornado inside him. "I'm sorry. If there was another way to stop him, then I wouldn't have come here. I know I don't have a right to ask, but I need your help."

"I can't."

"You can't? Convince me why," Weston snapped. "Because I'm not getting this. You must want this killer off the street. It's the only way you'll ever be truly safe."

Addie opened her mouth. Closed it. And she stared at him. "I'd planned on telling you. Not like this. But if I ever saw you again, I intended to tell you."

There was a new emotion in her voice and on her face. One that Weston couldn't quite put his finger on. "Tell me what?" he asked.

She dragged in a long breath and straightened her shoulders. "I can't be bait for the Moonlight Strangler because I can't risk being hurt." Addie took another deep breath. "I'm three months pregnant. And the baby is *yours*."

Don't miss
LONE WOLF LAWMAN
by USA TODAY *bestselling author Delores Fossen,*
available August 2015 wherever
Harlequin Intrigue® books and ebooks are sold.

www.Harlequin.com

HIEXP1015